RAFFI

PROHAERESIUS

TRANSLATED BY
KIMBERLEY MCFARLANE &
BEYON MILOYAN

SOPHENE BOOKS

LOS ANGELES

Published by Sophene 2022

Prohaeresius was first published in 1884 in Tiflis.
This translation was made from the original issues of *Aghbyur*,
in which *Prohaeresius* («*Պապոյր Հայկազն*») was originally published.

www.sophenebooks.com
www.sophenearmenianlibrary.com

ISBN-13: 978-1-925937-88-6

PROHAERESIUS

Hakob Melik Hakobian, better known as Raffi, was born in the Persian village of Payajuk in 1835 to a family of wealthy merchants. He was educated in Tbilisi, before he took over the family textile business. Thereafter, he taught and travelled extensively throughout Armenia, Transcaucasia, and Iran, and dedicated his life to writing. Raffi is among Armenia's literary treasures. He wrote over a dozen novels, short stories and poems, and pioneered the Armenian historical novel.

Originally published in 1884 in the Armenian language, *Prohaeresius* takes the reader to late antiquity Athens to introduce the Greco-Armenian philosopher, Prohaeresius. Little known to the modern world, Prohaeresius was among the most famed philosophers and orators of his day, with statues erected in his honor in Athens and Rome, and honors from the Byzantine court. Prohaeresius was also an illustrious and sought-after educator, teaching Saints Basil of Caesarea and Gregory the Theologian. Here, Raffi imagines a meeting between Prohaeresius and the Father of Armenian Literature, Movses Khorenatsi, where Movses implores Prohaeresius to return to Armenia to help the country face grave dangers. Interspersed with lines from ancient Armenian historical sources, this edition includes the first translation of *Prohaeresius*, the original Armenian text and "The Life of Prohaeresius," the only surviving contemporary biography of Prohaeresius by his student Eunapius (translated from Ancient Greek).

CONTENTS

Translators' Preface

The decade of 1880 was among the most ominous in Armenian history. The 1870s had concluded with the Russo-Turkish War of 1877-78, in which many Armenians perished or were sent away from their homes in exile. The year 1877 also witnessed Sheikh Jalaleddin's massacre of the Ottoman Armenians in the region of Van. The local and central Ottoman authorities alike had failed to punish or even condemn this atrocity, causing British war correspondent Charles Norman to place part of the responsibility on the Ottoman authorities.[1] In 1880, Raffi published his most renowned novel inspired by these events (*The Fool: Adventures in the Last Russo-Turkish War*). The book provided a powerful warning to Ottoman Armenians that the much deadlier consequences of this war were yet to come.

It is against this background that *Prohaeresius* was first published in 1884 in the literary journal *Aghbyur* in five monthly installments. The novella reflects the spirit of the Armenian national awakening that grew in response to the rise of Turkish nationalism over the preceding decades, and during which many Armenians had assimilated into Turkish culture and many more were losing their language and leaving their homeland to pursue wealth

---

1 See *Armenia and the Campaign of 1877* by Charles Norman.

and opportunities in metropolitan centers. This situation left the Ottoman Armenians (particularly those living in Cilicia and the Armenian plateau and highlands) in an increasingly precarious situation that Raffi was all too aware of:

> *We failed to recognize present-day Armenia for what it is. We only recognized by name a few of its ancient historians, and we imagined still a land with Tigrans, Arams, Vahakns, Vartans, and Nerseses. We imagined populous cities in which artisanship and commerce flourished and bestowed the country with wealth. We imagined its wealthy villages and fertile fields, whose yield filled the storehouses of the Armenian with all of God's blessings. We believed that the majority of the population here consisted of Armenians, who were leading lives of peace and prosperity on their native land. But we did not know that entire Armenian provinces were being stripped of Armenians, either because they were threatened by destitution or because they were forced to accept Islam. We did not know that instead of living Armenians, we would find either living corpses or vast graveyards. We did not know that our religion, which we consider the pillar of our national existence, had become extinct and in its place only ruins of once splendid churches and monasteries*

remained. We did not know that our language, the sacred inheritance of the people, had been lost, and that today the Armenian either speaks Kurdish or Turkish. We did not know that many among today's brave Kurds, who have become the scourge of God for Armenians, were fifty or a hundred years ago our brothers by blood, who spoke our language and prayed in our churches. In short, we knew nothing of modern Armenia, and it was not yet obvious to us that the scattered ruins of Armenia, owing to bitter circumstances and the heavy yoke of slavery, had decayed so much and become so obscene, that having lost its finest characteristics, had acquired in their place meanness, littleness, timidity, and deceitfulness…

The great powers of the world gathered in Constantinople. The Patriarch resided there—the head of the people—yet we never took into consideration the body. There, we had a National Representative Council that was occupied with intrigues and insignificant issues. There, we had educated youth, who made the shores of the Bosporus echo with Armenian songs on our national holidays; who had no idea that at that very moment, blood and tears were being shed in Armenia. There, we had the press that ignored the conditions in which the Armenians were living on their native land, occupied instead

*with the doings of foreigners. There, we had
schools that produced no teachers for Armenia. We had the theater that did not once
portray the unfortunate circumstances of the
Armenians but served its audience with the
kitchen filth of France. There, we had the
leaders of our people, who were flattering
the arbitrators of the Ottoman Porte to take
glory for themselves. We had the material
strength—money, which the wealthy used
to decorate their palaces, while not a single
dollar was spent on Armenia. In short, we
held the tiller of the prosperity of our people
in our own hands, it would seem, to mis-
guide it with evil thoughts and to lead it
toward destruction.*

It was due to a growing recognition of such
unfortunate circumstances that had grown increasingly dire over the course of prior decades that new
generations of Armenians started to found schools,
newspapers, periodicals, and printing presses. This
led to an outpouring of literature in the Modern
Armenian (*"Ashkharhabar"*) vernacular, enabling
Armenian literature to be widely disseminated and
read for the first time in history. These activities
were based largely in Constantinople, Tiflis, Vien-
na, and Venice. In 1858, Khachatur Abovian wrote
the first novel in this new vernacular (*Wounds of
Armenia*). By the 1860s, Raffi had begun writing periodicals for various Armenian journals and

newspapers, including Grigor Artsruni's newspaper *Mshak*, founded in Tiflis in 1872. Grigor, having just returned to Tiflis with a doctorate from the University of Heidelberg, commissioned Raffi to write a series entitled "*Travels through Persia*" about the living conditions of Armenians there. By the time *Prohaeresius* was published in 1884, Raffi had made a name for himself, his works now having been read by Armenians from Iran and Russia to Constantinople.

—

Prohaeresius is the eponym of the 4th century Armenian philosopher. It is the first of Raffi's two novels set in ancient Armenia, and the only one to make extensive use of Classical Armenian historical sources. As such, a translator of this novel faces many challenges. Whereas Raffi's contemporary novels are renowned for their rich descriptive elements of the lives and customs of the people, the author of a work set in ancient Armenia does not have a lot of material to work with in this respect. What little we know in regard to Prohaeresius' life comes down to us from his sole biography authored by his student, Eunapius. As Raffi himself describes in Chapter 4 of the book:

> *Among his many students, the most distin-*
> *guished became the great Basil, who held*

the renowned Bishopric of Caesarea,[2] and Saint Gregory the Theologian,[3] who with his voluminous works is eminent in Greek literature. To the latter's works belong Prohaeresius' epitaph. Also among his students was the young Eunapius, who wrote his dear teacher's biography.

Raffi's descriptions of Prohaeresius' life are most faithful to Eunapius' account, an English translation of which (from the Ancient Greek) can be found at the end of this book. If little is known today about the life of Prohaeresius, then surprisingly even less is known about the famed "Father of Armenian Literature" Movses Khorenatsi, who is a main character in this story. In fact, there even remains controversy about whether Khorenatsi was, in fact, a 5th century author (or, about how much of his *History* can be attributed to the 5th century Khorenatsi). Finally, some liberties were taken in rendering the Grabar translations of the excerpts that feature in the epigraphs and footnotes of *Prohaeresius,* in hopes of better situating them in the context of the story. The original quotations can be found in the original Armenian edition of the text in this book, which we have kept in Classical Orthography as it was originally composed.

---

2 St. Basil of Caesarea (330-379).
3 St. Gregory of Nazianzus (329-390).

There are numerous ways to read *Prohaeresius*. The first of these is as a semi-biographical account of the life of the Armenian philosopher, based faithfully on Eunapius' account, and of the life of Movses Khorenatsi, from what little autobiographical information he yielded in his *History*. The second way to read the book is through the eyes of a 19th century Armenian in the middle of a national awakening and on the eve of the Armenian Genocide. Raffi, one of the major figures of that awakening, tried uniting his nation against the grave threats of genocide that he saw before them—and that would indeed befall them just a decade later with the start of the Hamidian massacres of 1894 to 1896. In this sense, Raffi is speaking in this book to all his contemporary "Prohaeresiuses" who were enjoying the fruits of living in faraway lands while their beloved nation was on the brink of ruin. Last but not least, one can read the book as a very brief introduction to Classic Armenian literature from the perspective of one of Armenia's literary greats.

Kimberley McFarlane
Beyon Miloyan

PROHAERESIUS

*Dedicated to my friend and professor at
The University of Breslau, Andreas Artsruni.*

CHAPTER I

N the fourth century, when many Armenian youths went to Athens to be educated, a young man lived in a small, rundown building on a street in the backwaters of the city. He lived in one of its most unadorned lower rooms, where the lack of air and light gave the impression of a tomb. There was no furniture in that basement. Its damp floor was covered with straw that served as a bed, along with several worn rugs. Looking in through the windows, parchment manuscripts made of thick hide were visible. The room was narrow and was made less bearable by the presence of the young man's friend, Hephaestion. The young man himself was known as Prohaeresius.

The street where the two young men were staying was inhabited by people who were so poor that they only worked for, and thought about, their daily bread, and for that reason they were not very interested in the intellectual work of the two young men, and did not even know what they did.

Only with their external appearance did the young men capture their neighbors' attention. Prohaeresius was strong, physically attractive, and had a handsome face. His biographer, Eunapius, claims that he was eight feet tall and appeared mighty even beside the tallest young men of his time. Conversely, Hephaestion was of an average height and had a pale, sickly face.

The two young men admired each other so much that between them there lived one heart, one soul, and one will. Although they each belonged to opposing nationalities, it was their shared understanding of philosophy that had made them fraternal. Prohaeresius was Armenian, and Hephaestion was Greek. They were both students.

Prohaeresius' Armenian name was Paruyr, and I will refer to him by this name.

Being united in one spirit, the two young men also shared in bitter poverty. Aside from a single coat and robe, they both had nothing else to wear out of doors. They took turns wearing that coat and robe; when one was attending a lecture, the other was obligated to stay at home. There was no limit to the laughter of their neighbors when Hephaestion's turn arrived—when little Hephaestion, wrapped in tall Paruyr's coat and robe, hurried toward the academy.

The landlady, who was the wife of a kind artisan, was not very fond of the young students. This dissatisfaction arose not only because they were unable to pay rent for months on end, but also because, many times, at night, strange noises were heard from their underground room, as though one of them was giving a spirited, passionate speech, and the other was responding with equal passion or posing questions. These debates would sometimes last all night and erupt in the narrow atmosphere of the dark basement until sunrise. The superstitious landlady considered them hysterical; thinking that they were conversing with spirits, she was always worried that her children were afraid and unable to sleep. Although the young men would vow not to raise their voices, they were unable to keep their promise. Their enthusiasm was uncontrollable. In their rhetorical training they always forgot their surroundings.

In this way, battling with life and poverty, the young students spent several years in the capital of philosophy and rhetoric, until Paruyr, with his surprising advancement, captured the attention of his teacher, Julianus of Cappadocia, who saw a bright future in his student.

When Julianus left Athens, many tried to inherit his pulpit. Five candidates were chosen.[1] The competition was stiff: Athens was divided into several parties and each endeavored to have their candidate succeed. Unfortunately, at that time, the Roman government stuck its repressive hand into that independent temple of knowledge. For that

---

1 Raffi footnotes this naming Paruyr, his friend Hephaestion, Epiphanius, Diophantus, and Parnassius.

reason, those who found acceptance were not the true intellectuals, but rather the frauds who flattered the government's tastes. Given this, the possibility of the just and incorruptible Paruyr being elected was completely hopeless.

But Paryur was very famous in the empire's states and provinces, and because many children from the states were sent to Athens for education, the states also had a voice. A large part of the East voted for Epiphanius, those from Arabia voted for Diophantus, and those who voted for Paruyr were all the Pontics and Bithynians, that part of the Hellespont and Asia that extended from Caria to Lydia, and the mountains of Pamphylia and Taurus. In those regions, Paruyr had the entire population. Hephaestion did not want to compete against his friend, so he left the field for Paruyr and departed from Athens. Paruyr's election succeeded, and the orator, with his hard work, rose from his dark basement to the pulpit of Athens' academy of philosophy and rhetoric.

With this fame, our orator inherited many enviers. His enemy orators tried with the most disgraceful means to harm him. Only Paruyr's powerful genius and iron will could long withstand their lowly collusion. But eventually the opposition reached such a level that they falsely accused him of civil crimes, and the local Roman governor exiled him from Athens.

With the bitterness of exile, he once more bore the bitterness of poverty; but he had long been used to the latter. Only the boredom of unemployment caused him suffering. They had exiled him to one of the uninhabited Greek islands.

Paruyr bore his troubles in exile for a long time, until the governor was removed and a new one was appointed in his place. The orator's friends then tried to return him from exile and were able to succeed.

Returning to Athens, Paruyr found that many of his friends had passed away. Two of their deaths gave great pain to his sentimental heart: one was his friend Hephaestion, and the other was his friend Tuscianus. The latter's biographer, Sutias, called him "the most powerful orator." And the biographer of our orator Paruyr, Eunapius, said that "Tuscianus was the only one worthy of being 'Prohaeresius,' if Prohaeresius had not existed…"

After returning to Athens, Paruyr's enemies were provoked once more, and again started to set traps for him. The new governor was pressed to organize a public debate and to invite Paruyr to compete against his opponents. The spectators gathered, with both sides represented. On one side was Paruyr; on the other, a group of orators. The governor himself was to provide the theme of the competition, and the orators needed to give improvisational speeches. Paruyr's adversaries resisted, saying that without being able to prepare in advance, they would not speak. The governor then approached Paruyr, who fearlessly took the pulpit and exclaimed that his adversaries should propose any theme they wished to speak on. They maliciously chose a theme that was not only inappropriate for an eloquent speech, but was also almost impossible to speak on in an improvisational way. But our orator did not despair; he only asked that the scribes record his speech, so that there would be no room for complaints afterward that he did not speak to each point, and he asked the audience not to distract him with their applause.

The speech was so magnificent and profound that the listeners forgot their promise, and they shook the arches of the amphitheater with their enthusiastic cheers and applause.

The scribes were barely able to follow the flow of his speech, which poured out of his lips like a mighty tide. When he finished, the audience gave him a more spirited cheer.

But Paruyr, to display the astonishing power of his acumen, asked the spectators if he may repeat his speech, so that the scribes could compare it with what they had written in case something was missing—and from the first word to the last, he started repeating the same exact speech. The scribes did not find a single difference; it was as though he had learned the speech that he had just improvised by heart, far in advance.

Paruyr won the competition. The audience gave him congratulatory handshakes, calling him Hermes, the god of Oration. The governor, with his especial rank, led him home with a soldierly parade and ceremonial pomp.

Paruyr spent his days of honor in the same house where he had spent his student days in bitter poverty. The only difference between his initial stay and current stay was that Athens' god of Oration, instead of living in the same underground room, was now staying in a small room on the upper floor. His way of life had remained the same—he reigned supreme in his modest room with the same Spartan lifestyle and the same moderation with his simplest pleasures. His historic coat and robe, which he and his dear friend Hephaestion had sometimes worn, were kept in the room as a valuable reminder of the fraternal and enthusiastic life of his student days in which he had endured every sacrifice. Now his simple landlady was no longer dissatisfied, no longer anxious; instead, she glowed with a special pride around her neighbors because an important man was living in her house.

The same day, when the public was walking through those impoverished streets of Athens singing their praises, when they were leading Paruyr with the honor of victory to his house, there was an unfamiliar stranger in the horde. He remained completely unnoticed in that crowd, even though his face and unusual clothing were not very inconspicuous.

The day passed, darkness fell, and the streets of the neighborhood were emptied of its people. But the stranger was still wandering alone there. A few times, he approached the house where the hero of the day lived, but observing that there were still people there, he did not enter.

He continued walking, waiting for the people to leave. He paced up and down the length of the street a hundred times, and each time he approached the door, he put his ear to the opening and heard voices again.

The day was starting to break, and the residents started transporting groceries toward the town center with their donkeys, but the man had still not left the street.

At around noon the next day, a new crowd made its way to the orator's house with merry cheer. The stranger mingled with the crowd. "What's happening?" he asked someone in the crowd. "They are taking the king's declaration," was the response.

One honor after another. The Emperor Constans had sent an invitation to the orator.

Hearing this, the stranger shook his head and went away.

CHAPTER II

Two days had passed when one night the stranger reappeared at the door of the orator's house. No sound was audible from inside. He started knocking on the door. The servant replied that his master was very tired, as it has been a few nights that he had gone without sleep; people were not giving him rest. At last he was preparing to relax and had ordered that no one be admitted entry. "Tell your master that I am his compatriot, and he will accept me," the stranger replied.

A minute later the door opened, and the stranger was invited to enter. The orator, without recognizing him, without asking who he was, only hearing that he was Armenian, went to embrace the stranger at the door.

The stranger was a young man, quite tall, and with a strong build; having spent a long time under the Egyptian sun, his radiant face had taken on an attractive copper complexion. His long hair with dense curls reached down to his shoulders, and he had wrapped his head with a patterned headband, the ends of which dangled down onto his broad shoulders. In his black eyes one could discern a deep sadness, which reflected upon his whole face. The orator immediately discerned that sorrowful grief when the visitor quietly, without speaking a single word, passed into the room and sat on the couch.

What did this mean? Everyone had been excitedly visiting him for days, expressing warm happiness for his success, yet his compatriot did not utter a word on the topic; it was as though he had not seen anything and did not know anything about it. His first words were thus:

"They won't disturb us here?"

"Why do you ask?" the orator replied.

"I have something to discuss privately with you."

"But first and foremost, I must know who you are."

The stranger introduced himself.

"I have heard about you..." the orator declared, happily approached him, and embraced him again.

When the stranger was assured that they were alone, that everyone at home had left, and especially that no one was able to understand their language, he said:

"It is past midnight—let us not lose time, let us talk about what we need to: I will not stay long, I must set out on a journey come morning."

"Where did you arrive here from?"

"From Rome. I went there from Egypt, and then I came here to stay temporarily for something, but the situation changed… I am no longer able to stay…"

"Why not?"

"I received bad news from our country; I am hurrying there." He said the words with a certain bitterness, which also evoked sadness in Paruyr.

"A country of tears and blood!" he exclaimed. "When have we ever heard favorable news from there?"

"Now conditions have gotten worse," the young man said. "Vramshapuh,[2] the source of illumination of Armenia and the king who advanced the nation, has already died. After that, the Arsacid dynasty briefly inherited a few insignificant kings, until someone more unworthy, the young Artashir,[3] became king. Misfortune used to come from outside, but it has now started to grow from within. The young king, with his fickle behavior, instigated the loathing of the Armenian nakharars[4] who, being even more mindless, approached the Persian king Bahram,[5] requesting that he overthrow Artashir and put a Persian marzban[6] in his place to govern Armenia. This was what the Persian king had long desired, and he

---

2 Vramshapuh (389-414).
3 Artaxias IV (422-428).
4 Nakharars were the highest-ranking nobles (lords) in Armenian society.
5 Bahram V (420-438).
6 *Marzban*, a Sasanian title for governors or military commanders of border provinces.

fulfilled the nakharars' wishes with great pleasure. All the efforts of our father, Sahak,[7] were fruitless, as he tried to restrain the mindlessness of the nakharars and to make them understand the great evil they were committing. However, they also betrayed Sahak, and by the hands of the Persian king deprived him of the Patriarchal throne.[8] And like that, the two pillars of Armenia—the monarchal throne and the Patriarchal Chair—were destroyed. Both Sahak and Artashir were exiled to Persia. Our ungoverned homeland is now in fatal distress: it is necessary to deliver assistance."

"With what?" Paruyr asked coldly. Rather than answering, the young man looked sharply at the orator's face, as though he wanted to say, 'Do you really not understand, with what?'

"With what?" the orator repeated. "Are you going to fight the Persians?"

"Why not! If it is necessary" the young man replied, visibly frustrated by the orator's coldness.

The orator, noticing this, said:

"Go, I compliment your aspiration."

The young man became more furious.

"Paruyr!" he exclaimed, "your Armenian blood is frozen, you are a lost man to our homeland. You are told of the great difficulties that are taking place

---

7 Sahak I Partev, Catholicos (388-439).
8 That is, the Catholicosal throne.

in our country and you listen cold-heartedly. You have changed, you have changed a lot. You, who a few days ago amazed all of Athens with your oration, now speak ill with the same tongue with which you once spoke to your parents. Your Hellenomania has developed so much that you have even changed your name; you used to call yourself Paruyr in your homeland, and here you call yourself Prohaeresius.

The orator felt those words. The young man continued:

"I am taking responsibility for scolding you, Paruyr, even though you are older than me and higher in rank. But do not forget you too were one of those young men, who left their homeland in the name of learning, who swore before our Patriarch Sahak and Mesrop,[9] to travel from country to country, to acquire a wealth of knowledge, and to return home to enlighten the citizens of our homeland. You, me, and all our friends, having made every sacrifice, went to Edessa,[10] Antioch, Byzantium, Alexandria, Rome, and Athens: we visited all the temples of knowledge and quenched our thirst. The grandness of our objective kindled our aspiration, and the nobility of our ideas gave us strength and power. We

---

9   Mesrop Mashtots, the creator of the Armenian alphabet (d. 440).
10 Edessa (Urfa).

all became renowned in our fields. My first cousin's friend David[11] competed in Byzantium, in the presence of Emperor Marcian,[12] and silenced all the philosophers with his boundless knowledge, earning him the name 'invincible philosopher.' Eznik,[13] Hovsep,[14] Ghevond,[15] and Koryun[16] impressed the Bishop Maximianus with their theological skill. My brother Mampre,[17] Yeghishe,[18] and Ghazar Parpec'i[19] were similarly celebrated as powerful theologians, and as deeply learned scholars. I am not mentioning many other young men who traveled west with the objective of completing their education and made surprising returns. Now many of these young men, hearing of their country's disasters, have returned to our

11 "David the Invincible is known for his philosophical pedigree and his most interesting works of translation." —Raffi

12 Marcian (450-457).

13 "Eznik of Kolb is known for his book, *Against the Sects*, in which he drew critical attention to the sham philosophizing of his day, principally the magian Persian element." —Raffi

14 "Hovsep, who went on to become the Catholicos of Armenians, assembled the meeting of Artashat and announced Vartan's war against Persian control." —Raffi

15 "Ghevond 'erets was known for his love of Armenia in the time of Vartan's war." —Raffi

16 "Koryun was one of the notable translators of the Bible; he then became Bishop of Georgia, before the Armenian and Georgian churches divided, and wrote the biography of his teacher Mesrop." —Raffi

17 "Mampre, whom they call 'the Decipherer,' is notable for his historical and grammatical works." —Raffi

18 "Yeghishe, besides his various works of holy exegesis, wrote the history of the Battle of Avarayr." —Raffi

19 "Ghazar Parpec'i is known for his interesting history of Armenians and his letter to Vahan Mamikonian, in which appears that time's dark-minded ecclesiastical persecution of the virtuous self-sacrificers." —Raffi

homeland, and the remainder are hurrying to return. They are taking a new weapon with them to rescue Armenia, and that is—enlightenment."

The orator, who listened to all this with deep concentration, slowly asked:

"You think that enlightenment will rescue Armenia?"

"I do not only think that, I am convinced of it," the young man responded with passion. "You have apparently forgotten about the unfortunate events that have recently occurred in our country. Armenia's only fortune was that the Patriarchal Chair was occupied by that genius of a man, our Father, Sahak Partev.[20] With an eagle's vision, he foresaw that terrifying danger that was threatening our homeland. He saw the looming fall of the Arsacid dynasty—saw that it would be divided among Greeks and Persians, one of which must be more harmful than the other. He also saw the misfortune that Saint Gregory the Illuminator's Patriarchal Chair would be inherited by frauds, greedy persons, and traitors. He saw the end of the two powerful protectors of the homeland: the spiritual and physical rulers. At that time a savior needed to arrive to offer assistance, to replenish the major loss that constituted the fall of our spiritual and

---

20 Sahak *Partev* (the Parthian), Catholicos (388-439).

physical rulers—and that rescue started to emerge in the people's education and enlightenment. That was the principal motive for every effort to be spent in spreading education in our country—education with our mother tongue."

The orator was listening and stroking his beard with his fingers. The young man continued:

"Our Patriarch Sahak's predecessors had placed the work of educating the population on limited and weak foundations. They had inserted Greek and Syriac education along with Christianity. Our first teachers were the Greeks and Assyrians; we wrote and read in their languages. Our Church also operated using foreign languages. We listened to biblical readings in either Greek or Syriac, while the Persians were trying to introduce their language as the official language of our schools and courts. Our Patriarch Sahak saw plainly that major trouble could arise from this. The mother language was progressively dying, and with that, the national culture—and this would be the real death of Armenia. The Armenian, by losing his language, would dissolve into, and disappear among, those people whose languages he was speaking. The magnitude of the danger was horrifying, and the great Patriarch worked to preempt it.

He knew that even if the Armenians lost their independence, renewal would be possible if the culture remained alive. But with the loss of language, Armenians would cease to exist as an independent people: they would become Greek, Assyrian, Persian, or any one of those people whose language they had come to speak. In order to preempt that danger, he took on the duty of educating the people. It was necessary to make everything Armenian; to make everything national. Our Patriarch Sahak, in all his plans, had an active man as a supporter: Mesrop. He hastened to invent a new alphabet for the Armenians, so that they would no longer have to write in the Greek, Syriac, or Persian script. They began using the same language to translate the Scripture, so that the Armenian language and script presides in the Church. They started to open schools and educate the youth in the Armenian script and language.

"The Greeks and Persians, who had already taken Armenia in their claws and were preparing to devour the nation—those two formidable empires could not fail to notice that mighty resistance that Armenia's far-sighted Patriarch was preparing to take before their insidious politics. The Greeks began preventing the opening of Armenian schools in the region of Armenia that was under their suzerainty. It must be evident to you how much persecution and how many negotiations our Patriarch Sahak Partev had with the royal court of the Byzantines, until Mesrop and his grandson Vartan were compelled to personally go to Byzantium and request permission from the emperor and the bishop Atticus[21] to open schools—an idea that received great resistance. The Persian government offered the same resistance, but with greater severity. They sent the malefactor Merujan,[22] an Armenian by race, who burnt our books and through his hands worked to insert Magian doctrine and the Iranian language into our newly established schools."

The orator continued to stroke his beard with his fingers. The young man went on:

"The competition between the Greek and Iranian powers was fierce but uneven. Well-prepared intervention was necessary in the eyes of our Patriarch Sahak and Mesrop, and it was with such intentions that they chose you, me, and their other high-caliber students, and sent them to Byzantium, Alexandria, Rome, and Athens to receive a high education. We passed through these cities so that, receiving a Grecian education, we could return to our homeland and fight them with their own weapons."

---

21 Atticus of Constantinople (406-425).
22 Merujan Artsruni, described in P'awstos Buzand's *History of the Armenians*.

"The means is appropriate to the objective," replied the orator, ceasing to play with his beard.

"But you should have also been one of those soldiers," replied the young man, looking straight into the orator's eyes. "That's why I came to you, so that we could return together."

The orator hesitated; he had not been anticipating that proposition and did not know how to respond.

The young man spoke:

"I understand and respect the reason for your silence and uneasiness, Paruyr, but I cannot agree with you. That honor, that fame you are enjoying here is blinding you. Relinquishing all of that and returning to your wretched homeland, where many sacrifices are being demanded from our active men—that is scaring you. Our friends David Anhaght,[23] Yeghishe, Yeznik, Ghazar P'arpec'i, Koryun, my brother Mamprē, Hovsep, Ghewond—in a word, all the students, who were dispersed across different countries—have now returned or are on the verge of returning. You and I remain. Let us go, let us not delay, our homeland is calling us. Let us spread knowledge and light to our country, let us open our compatriots' eyes, let us teach them to understand their evil and their good, to

---

23 *David Anhaght:* "David the Invincible".

understand what kind of abyss they are standing on the edge of—that, if they were to fall in, they will vanish for eternity. You have such a powerful genius that by staying here, I have come to believe, you will rise all the more, and perhaps rise to be among the best philosophers and orators of our time. But what good does that have for your homeland?

"Humanity would benefit from that," the orator replied following a long silence. "By serving knowledge, I am at once serving the entire world."

"That is true," the young man replied, in a somewhat fervent manner. "But do you not accept that you have a certain obligation toward your homeland and toward your compatriots?"

"I accept that, but my objective is broad. You and others work in small areas, by which I mean to say in the individual pockets of humanity that you call 'nations'. My homeland is the entire world, and my compatriots are all mankind."

The fiery young man stood up, furious:

"That's hypocritical reasoning, Paryur," he said, his mighty voice breaking in extreme indignation. "Those of you who say such things are Pharisees of knowledge. In order to disparage the particular you always speak in general terms, in the same way that those who default on paying their own debts preach ownership for all. I had hoped that you would not need me to speak much; rather, that hearing of the difficult situation in your homeland, you would have befriended me and we could have left Athens this morning. But I have spoken excessively in vain, and it has been a loss to me. It is not the love of wisdom and the idea of universal enlightenment that tie you to Athens, but lowly honors and that piece of parchment on your desk...."

With those words, the young man extended his hand and took the emperor's edict that the orator had received that day, and rising, said:

"Here, the piece of parchment that cajoles you. The emperor of the East and West invites you to him with that decree. On the other hand, your unfortunate homeland calls to you through my words. You reject its call, and that is why you are unworthy of calling yourself a child of Armenia."

With those last words, the young man left. The orator remained stupefied, as though he had been struck by lightning. The young man was Movses Khorenatsi.

CHAPTER III

*"And while they [Sahak and Mesrop] hoped for
our return to a love of honor in my most learned
wisdom and perfect aptitude, we all quickly head-
ed for Byzantium, hoping to dance at weddings
with intrepid swiftness and to sing wedding songs.
Now, instead of such festivities, I lament over their
graves with a sigh of pity—where I did not arrive
in time to see them close their eyes and to hear their
final words and blessing[s]."*

– Khorenatsi

The darkness of night enclosed the Ararat Plain.
Not a single light was visible from the solitude of
Saint Mesrop's dwelling in Oshakan village. Every
creature was deeply asleep, and everything was im-
mersed in a deafening silence. Not even the endless
psalmody of the nocturnal ascetics was heard; only
an oil lantern was smoking in a chapel, and, like
the sorrowful expression of a sad soul, was spreading its dim light around itself.

In the chapel, an epitaph was inscribed. The
light of the lantern was spilling directly upon it,
making the unadorned carving visible. The epitaph was composed of black rock, as though it was
figuratively proclaiming the spiritual bitterness of

the great man to whom it was inscribed, which descended into the mournful tomb full of inconsolable affliction.

Near the epitaph, a man was bowed on his knees in prostration on the bare floor. His head was resting on the cold, flat tombstone, and his long, bountiful hair covered its black surface. He was immobile in that position, and so too were his arms, with which he was embracing the epitaph. No utterance or groan were emitted from the mourner's sad, quiet gift of lamentation; only mild streams of tears flowed from his half-covered eyes onto the cold rock.

For a long time, sprawled over the floor, he embraced the epitaph in that way—for a long time, with his forehead like that on the cold rock, he clung to it, as though he was trying to call up the phantom of that great departed person, trying to see him, to speak to him, and pour out his heart's sorrows before him.

Sprawled like that, he was lamenting in silence, until the doleful sounds of the early morning call from the solitary bell tower became audible. The mild ringing snapped him out of his spiritual throes. He raised his head and looked around in marked horror. The day was dawning… it was as though he was afraid they would see him here. He rose to his feet…

Who was the nocturnal visitor spilling his bitter tears over the tombstone?

"Peace be upon your sacred bones, O blessed Father!" he exclaimed, his sorrowful glance lingering on the epitaph. "Returning to his homeland after long travels, your unfortunate student had great hopes of finding solace in your embrace and to comfort you. But he did not become worthy of your pleasant company, did not hear a final blessing from your lips, and did not close with his own hands those sharp eyes which, seeing those calamities near and far to our homeland, instead of crying, put every effort into finding cures. According to your commands, I went from country to country, city to city, visited all the temples of knowledge, and return to our homeland full of erudition. But who will hereafter value that intellectual stock that I have brought from foreign countries?[24] Only you and your majestic associate (Sahak) understood that which is the true light and correct instruction. Your cruel death simultaneously put out those two suns, and now darkness governs the land of the Armenians. The good have left and the wicked are replacing them. The Assyrians have inherited our

---

24 "Who, hereafter, will respect our education; who will delight in the advancement of this student, who will declare his fatherly joy...?" –Khorenatsi

Patriarchal throne of the Holy Illuminator,[25] and Armenian Patriarchs are working to make us ingratiate ourselves to the despotic Persian court, rather than to the church of Jesus Christ.[26]

Our current teachers,[27] who needed to give spiritual and moral guidance to the people, who needed to teach them what is real and just, are themselves further confusing the people. They are at once ignorant and vain. They have received rank and status without having any intellectual and moral worth. They are elected more by money than due to the Holy Spirit, and they are avaricious and envious for that reason. Christian virtue is absent in them and abandoning their good nature, in which God resides, they have become wolves and are devouring their flock. Our monks[28]—our monks, who needed to set an example of our ardent faith and brotherhood to the people, who needed to ignite in them the spirit of love and

---

25   "Holy Illuminator", i.e., St. Gregory the Illuminator, the patron saint of Armenia. The Assyrian inheritance of the Patriarchal Chair refers to the two Assyrian bishops, Brkisho and Samuel, who served as Catholicoi of the Armenian church for 9 years after St. Sahak's abdication in 428.

26   "I pity you, church of Armenia, obscured of your luster and deprived of your shepherd and his companion [the Catholicos and King]. I no longer see your rational flock in the wild foliage and nourished by tranquil waters, and no longer taking caution from wolves by gathering [them] in your barns but dispersing [them] to the wilderness and precipices." —Khorenatsi

27   "The ignorant and self-indulgent teachers took honor by themselves and not called by God; chosen by silver and not by the Spirit; money-loving and envious—they have abandoned gentleness, where God resides, and have become wolves who devour their flock." —Khorenatsi

28   "[Our] monks are hypocritical, ostentatious, vainglorious and lovers of honors rather than lovers of God." –Khorenatsi

brotherhood—they are sowing yet more the seeds of disunion. They are deceiving the people with the hypocrisy of the Pharisees, with the guise of piety, but within they are vainglorious and lovers of honors, rather than God-loving. Pretending to be detached from the pleasures of the world and from communication with man, they enjoy the whole world within the quiet walls of their monasteries. Our clergy,[29] who needed to defend rights and justice among the people, who needed to do so for the reformation of the church, are themselves eroding its foundations. Those lazy, careless church administrators are spending their time in the entertainment of exchanging gossip and jokes. Their knowledge and pedagogical teachings are detestable, and dear is their solicitation of advice. Simony, through the hands of those scroungers, has reached extreme shamelessness. For worthless Mammon, every year they fill the good-for-nothing church officials' ranks! What kind of generation is currently being prepared at the hands of these disorderly instructors? What sort of a condition are the students in our schools being subjected to?[30] Our former love for true knowledge and our former fervency for a useful education no longer remain.

---

29 "The clergy are proud, vain, babblers, lazy, haters of wonders and words of instruction, lovers of marketplaces and buffoonery." –Khorenatsi
30 "The students are lazy to learn and eager to teach—[they] become theologians before they are examined." –Khorenatsi

Our schools are educating a lazy, empty-minded generation, which has yet to learn anything yet attempts to give the appearance of popular theologians who, remaining completely ignorant in their interpretation of the Scripture, begin to instruct others. The seminary, the antechamber of the holy church, is no longer sowing pure and sacred seeds in the hearts of the youth, such that in the future they will become the faithful children of the church and their homeland, and will recognize their debt to the heavens and to the world—to humanity. Today's seminaries, on the contrary, are suffocating, obliterating in the youths' hearts those tender buds that, sprouting in the future and blooming, could have yielded gracious fruit…

He paused for a while and after a momentary silence continued:

"Behold, the work of the church's administration and the spiritual and intellectual education of the people are in the hands of such individuals. And as for us? We are now considered sectarians.[31] The ignorant, dimwitted, and hypocritical clergy are persecuting us. They consider our literary works

---

31 "So they say, '*He is a sectarian.*' And this they assert to all in haste, and have the weak-minded believe that my teaching is lacking in grace."
—Ghazar Parpec'i

to be harmful;[32] our education and instruction they regard as misleading. There is not one lord, not one leader, to subdue those envious, evil-minded, gowned slanderers,[33] who fraudulently provoke the naïve people against us and obstruct our actions. You, O blessed father, along with your mighty associate (St. Sahak), created a new generation of ecclesiastics. They were not few in number. Not being satisfied with the education that they had received under your tutelage, you and your great associate sent them to foreign lands to improve their education. They went and returned having learned much. But what became their demise? The dim-witted clergy did not allow many of them to enter the borders of their native land,[34] and those who did return were persecuted… Now, those self-sacrificing cultivators of our homeland live in concealment and only work in secret. They do not have

---

32 "The blessed philosopher Movses, who, while verily still in the flesh, was all the while among the citizens of the heavenly host. Did the Armenian monks not, indeed, persecute him from place to place? Did they not, in their ignorance, call his illuminating and ignorance-expelling writings deceptive…?" —Ghazar Parpec'i

33 "Who will condemn the audacity of those who rise up to oppose the correct teachings, who are broken and destroyed by every word, who change many teachers and many books… Who will stop their mouths and scold them, and comfort us with praise, and restrict speech and silence (in due measure)?" —Khorenatsi

34 "The pure and well-respected hope, lord Khosrovik, had not yet reached our borders, when they heard that he was on his way, and went upon him armed, as though against an enemy, saying 'Behold, where is the other translator going?' And the blessed one [Khosrovik], hearing from afar the ominous rustling of the bows, prayed to the Most High, and immediately ceded to their demand; others, and not us, became worthy of receiving his desirable relics." –Ghazar Parpec'i

the boldness to impart the knowledge they brought from abroad to the people. The name "translator" with respect to us has become a derisive and ignominious name in the mouths of the anachromaniacal clergy. We were putting in every bit of effort and continue to do so in order for the Armenian to speak the Armenian language in his home, and for the Armenian to pray in the Armenian language in God's home—we were working, and are still working, to Armenianize everything, to give everything an ethnic character—we translated all the Scriptures with the alphabet you created, and we were trying to bring those God-given letters into Armenian life and usage—we put all our efforts to work to keep our seminaries and churches free of the harmful influence of the insidious Greeks, the wicked Persians, and the deceptive Assyrians—we are now being persecuted for our works, and being persecuted by whom? Our own kind…

While pronouncing those last words, his voice choked up from agitation and the fire of wrath shone in his eyes.

"Look, holy father, look with the eyes of your soul; see my sorrowful condition. The traveling staff in my hand, the sack over my shoulders, the ragged clothes over my body, like a pitiable beggar—I have come and arrived here. Our monasteries, which, serving as inns, are found full of foreign travelers and nourishing sustenance, our monasteries would not even give me a corner to stay the night, and there were many that I did not even dare to enter, so that I would not fall into the snares of malevolent people… I have gone hungry for many days, and many times I have been compelled to approach the doors of gracious villagers and request a morsel of food. I have concealed who I am and what I do… and that man who impressed the emperor Marcianus at Byzantium with his wisdom and enjoyed his hospitality—now that sufferer does not dare to show his face in his own native land."

Jolts of anger were again perceptible on his furious face, which transformed into a calmer gentleness after a moment's silence.

"But all those persecutions cannot discourage me, or dispirit me and my friends. As self-sacrificing soldiers, we have vowed to battle darkness and ignorance, vowed to battle the betrayal and evils of the mercantile clergy; the clergy who destroyed our royal throne and have now turned our Patriarchal Chair into a tool through the hands of the ruinous Persians to eliminate our remaining powers in our own land…"

He kneeled down again next to the epitaph and his lips left a kiss on the cold headstone.

"I take an oath on this holy epitaph," he proclaimed, "and repeat my vow, which will remain firm until the last breath of my life. Persecution and difficulties cannot kill that spirit that you, O blessed father, inspired in my heart. I will always remain faithful in that great mission, for which I was called upon as an apostle to serve. Your noble aim to rescue our native land through teaching and illumination needs to be realized. That foundation, which you laid with your proficient hands, my friends and I will continue to build upon. Our unfortunate land has outlasted you, but your spirit and grand vision remain alive in our hearts. You and your mighty associate left behind a small and unprotected group of students, it is true; but that insignificant group in its minority will still be great and powerful, because it was inspired by noble ideas pertaining to all our people…"

The monastic bells started ringing louder and louder. The dawn sky turned a purple hue. The sounds of newly risen birds outside were audible.

The stranger kissed the tombstone again and again, and for the last time, casting his sad glance on the black headstone, he took his staff and sack and carefully went out of the chapel.

The early morning service was being conducted in the monastery. The monks were praying. The old sexton, sitting alone opposite the church door and quite satisfied with his state, was looking out at the heights of the bell tower, atop which the pigeons were courting each other. One of the attendants was sweeping the yard.

The sexton saw the stranger from afar. His traveler's staff, the sack tied around his waist, and his tattered clothes gave the sexton reason to think that the traveler must be a beggar who had sheltered in the monastery at night. But one thing caused him doubt—why was the traveler leaving the monastery early like this, without going into church or at least kissing its door? He called the attendant sweeping the yard near him and asked:

"Did you see that beggar?"

"I saw," the attendant replied, scratching his side. "He came out from St. Mesrop's chapel."

"St. Mesrop's chapel?" the sexton repeated, surprised. "What was he up to there?"

"What else could he have been up to?" the attendant replied, still scratching his side. "He seems to have entered to pay his respects at the tomb of his old teacher.

"Who was he?"

"You didn't recognize him?"

"Hundreds of beggars come here—how could you recognize him?"

"He was not a beggar."

"Who was he?"

"Movses."

"Movses who?"

"Khorenatsi."

The sexton remained confused.

"Did you see him with your own eyes? Did you recognize him? Did you speak to him?"

"Of course I saw him—how could I not see him!" the attendant replied, now scratching his opposite side. "I saw him with my own two eyes, I recognized him well, but he didn't talk to me. I have known him since he was a boy this big."

While speaking these last words, he held his hand at an arm's length off the ground to indicate his height.

The sexton, deep in thought, rubbed his forehead with his hand and said in a barely audible voice:

"Our clerics are looking for him…"

"The devil himself won't be able to find him now."

"Why not?"

"Don't you know that the newly arrived heretical vardapets from Rome are all like sorcerers?"

CHAPTER IV

Boast greatly no longer with your head held high Cecropia,

It is not right to measure a torch against the light of the sun,

Nor to pit a mortal against Prohaeresius in rhetoric,

Who vanquished the world with his words of oration.

Attica shook with unexpected thunder:

But the academies of outspoken intellectuals

Yielded to Prohaeresius, and gave way to what was fated.

The resplendent glory of Athens was marred when he passed,

In bitterness upon its deathbed.

Flee hereafter from Cecropia, young apprentices!

—Gregory the Theologian[35]

---

35 Gregory the Theologian (Gregory Nazianzen)'s epitaph for his teacher, Prohaeresius.

A tall man with an august face freely frequented emperor Constans' luxurious court. The courtiers stood before him with the highest esteem and greeted him with deep respect.

He was neither a distinguished general nor a ruler of lands. He was neither a vassal nor a prince. His plain and simple clothing did not indicate whether he was someone who had been endowed with worldly ranks. At times, he was seen entering the palace barefoot; at times without a hat, and his long hair was tied with an ordinary headband. Yet still every head bowed before him.

Disregarding worldly ranks in this heedless manner, only two types of persons enter the palace of the mighty—the prophet and the philosopher. This man was a philosopher and an orator.

He had a seat at the most respectable place at the emperor's table. This man's presence at this table, around which the kings of other lands were served, bestowed it with great honor. But that abundant table—which was full of the world's most precious blessings, and on which the world's most prized foods and drinks were placed on gold and silverware—that table did not appetize him. He drank plain water and ate dry bread with fresh fruit.

The man was a guest in Rome. He animated the emperor's palace with his intelligent, eloquent speech, and gave counsel and spirit to the queen with his speeches. Everyone marveled with great delight that Cicero had resurrected; everyone, from the magistrates of the Senate to the last citizen, was eager to hear his instruction.

For a whole six months, he distributed intellectual and spiritual nourishment to Rome, and when time came to leave, the city decided to eternalize his memory with a statue honoring him.

The copper statue stood in one of the more conspicuous public squares of the city and resembled the orator in size and appearance. The unveiling took place in the most illustrious fashion, in accordance with Rome's festive taste. When they lifted the veil, the description on the base of the statue read:

From Rome, the queen,
to the king of eloquence.

In those same days, when all the doors of the emperor's palace were open before the orator, and when Prohaeresius was boldly coming and going as an honorable guest, two Easterners lingered before the palace doors in the public square every day. From their clothes, weapons, and insignia it appeared that the strangers were not commoners—rather, they were vassal kings or ruling princes from foreign lands. Each of them had a group of guards and servants with him, and each donned red shoes and red bottoms, which was a sign of their lordly status. It had been over one week that those strangers had appeared before those palace doors, but they had still not entered the royal court nor presented themselves to the emperor, even though they had come expressly for that purpose. They had only met with the vassal of Asia Minor several times, who constantly gave them hope that he would arrange for them to meet the emperor; but the days were passing, and their request continued to go unfulfilled. When the foreigners insisted that they must meet with the emperor, the vassal said sarcastically, "At the emperor's court, even kings are made to wait months or years, but you Armenians, it seems you are impatient…"

The two foreign princes appeared at around the same time that the orator received his great honor, after the celebration of the unveiling of the statue had passed, and he was preparing to leave Rome. Without revealing who they were and with what objective they had come, they gave him a letter from the Catholicos of the Armenians, St. Vrtanes. Following the customary Patriarchal blessings and well wishes, the letter started with these words:

"It is a great honor and pride for Armenians and Armenia that one of its children is astonishing all the East and West with his reason, and with his genius is enjoying the high honors of the palace of the august emperor of Rome. Not even those conquerors who extended the borders of the Roman empire to Asia and Africa had merited such an honor.

"The friendly relations between our mighty king Trdat and the father of Rome's emperor, Constantine the Great, must be evident to you. It must also be evident to you that the 'pact of alliance',[36] which was written and sealed between those two monarchs as a condition of reciprocal friendship and assistance, intended to remain steadfast from generation to generation. That covenant was maintained throughout Trdat's lifetime, and Armenia became a strong rampart against the Persians, not allowing them to easily attack the borders of the Roman empire.

"Trdat was a formidable weapon against the enemies of our homeland, and throughout his entire reign, all of Persia and their king Shapur were kept in consternation. He died and our land went into inconsolable grief.

---

36 For a review of the pact between Trdat and Constantine, see Thomson, R. (1997). Constantine and Trdat in Armenian tradition. *Acta Orientalia Academiae Scientiarum Hungaricae, 50,* 277-289.

"Armenia is now floundering in anarchy. The nakharars are divided and in internal strife. Sanatruk has become the independent king of Paytakaran.[37] Some of the nakharars, following his example, are trying to extend their own dominions. Bakur, the bidaxš[38] of Artsni, has broken away from the union of the Armenian nakharars and is pursuing the same objective. The enemy, taking advantage of our internal strife, is aggravating us from all sides. Shapur, in order to quench the thirst of an old vengeance, like a furious brute, has turned our country to ruins. Armenia's throne has been vacated for a king from his line. There has not been a great man, not a leader, who has been able to collect all the divided powers and combine their forces against the enemy. Armenia is in a state of dissolution. Your one word would be enough to rescue our land from existential danger. For the love of our people, for the love of our homeland, intercede on our behalf to the emperor, remind him of our old pact, and request his help for installing Khosrov as king in place of his father Trdat. With that, you will have accomplished your holy duty toward your unfortunate homeland and toward your people, who boast about you and bestow great respect upon you, by calling you their

---

37 The easternmost province of Armenia.
38 A high-ranking state minister in Sasanian Iran.

son.

"In addition to that pact, a separate letter was written by us and our lords to the emperor with royal offerings, and was sent to Mar, the prince of Sophene, by the hand of Gag, prince of Hashteank. These princes will explain to you what we have omitted from our letter."[39]

Not one nerve or muscle moved in the orator's cold countenance while reading that pitiable letter. He put the letter aside and fell into thought, like a man deep in contemplation while writing.

"You have still not met the emperor?" he asked, turning toward the two princes.

"No, despite having asked the courtiers many times," they replied.

"And is the emperor aware of your arrival?"

"Certainly, he must be aware; we did not come empty-handed, we came bearing royal gifts, which they presented to the emperor. Our Patriarch Vrtanes has also written to you about that."

"Yes, he has… so now what is the difficulty?"

"Truly, nothing," the prince of Hashteank replied. "What difficulty would we bear, when we have a respected man like you in the emperor's palace? Your one word would suffice for the emperor

---

39 "Grasping this, the Armenian nakharars met with Vrtanes the Great and sent two of their honorable princes—Mar, prince of Sophene, and Gag, prince of Hashteank—to the capital city to the caesar Constantine, son of Constantinus, with gifts and a letter." —Khorenatsi

to fulfill our request. Now the success of our ambassadorial visit depends on you."

"On me…?" the orator asked, confused. "But I don't know how appropriate my intervention would be…"

The two princes were shocked; they were not expecting such a response.

"What are you doubtful of?" the prince of Sophene asked.

"Given that I am not involved in politics, it is not entirely clear to me what vision or objective the emperor has with the Armenian throne."

The prince of Sophene, who was more irritable than his companion, replied somewhat angrily:

"The emperor's objectives can be either advantageous or disadvantageous to Armenia; in other words, he either wishes for Armenia's throne to be retained, or he wishes for it to be eradicated and for Armenia to turn into a state of the Roman empire. Tell us, please, what you would do if the emperor's objective were the latter?"

"I would acquiesce to his will."

"And if the emperor wished to defend Armenia?"

"Then I would intervene."

"As much as your honest confession is praiseworthy," the prince of Hashteank interjected, "your flattery to the emperor is that much more reprehensible. If it were a Roman saying this, I would have praised his patriotism. If a Roman had said to me, 'I will observe my emperor's wish, and if he intends to integrate Armenia, then I will wish for the same, or if the emperor decides to defend an independent Armenia, I will also wish for the same,' he would not anger me with such a judgment. But when an Armenian says that, he loses all significance in my eyes, however great he was."

The orator was not injured in the slightest by those sharp words; he was an extremely forgiving man. His cold countenance seemed to express the words, 'You are getting angry in vain, prince, what am I guilty of? That I have been unfortunate to be born an Armenian…?' But he did not speak those words, and instead replied very calmly:

"You completely misunderstood what I said, prince. I would have praised Armenia with greater conviction if I had been a Roman. But being Armenian, my tongue impedes me. I do not wish to put him in a difficult situation, though I know for certain that he would acquiesce to my request. However, I have not been in the habit of requesting anything from him that could subject him to the slightest vexation; I do not allow myself to put my faith and love toward the emperor to evil ends."

"That would have been legitimate if the issue pertained to you or your personal profits, but the issue here pertains to the life and death of our homeland," the prince of Hashteank noted.

"That is what subjects me to difficulty," the orator replied with a certain self-satisfaction, as though the subject of debate had already been settled. "My homeland is closer to me than some foreign country; from there we reach the plain conclusion that advocating for my homeland is one and the same as advocating for myself. But I am not in the habit of advocating on my own behalf. I would have mediated much more easily if Armenia had been a foreign country to me."

The two princes angrily stood up again.

"Our conversation is over," they said. "Now everything is clear to us. You are selfish to the highest degree, Paruyr. You do not wish to sacrifice your love of self for your homeland. You fear that you will appear patriotic in the emperor's eyes because that could subject you to suspicion. But know, Paruyr, that if the emperor has the heart of a Roman, he respects patriotism in every individual. He considers as vile, low, and cowardly the man who remains coldhearted toward the misfortunes faced by his homeland…"

The two princes departed.

A good-hearted smile appeared on the orator's face, like those smiles that appear on the faces of adults when they are judged by children.

"Simple-minded people," he said, after the princes departed. "Every despot sees patriotism as permissible for himself and his subjects, but finds it unbearable for foreigners…"

The next day, the orator needed to leave Rome. He was preparing to present himself before the emperor and deliver his parting address. A group of high-ranking courtiers were leading him to the royal court. The emperor admitted him with many congratulations, while also expressing his regret for being deprived of his dear guest's agreeable company.

"I thank you, Prohaeresius," the sovereign of the world said, extending his hand. "With your presence in my palace, you sweetened many hours of my troubles, and with your wisdom in my palace, you raised the standard of the rhetorical stage. The city fulfilled its debt of appreciation and erected a statue in your name. It remains for me to do the same. Request from me whatever you wish. I am ready to bring it to fruition."

Paruyr had the most favorable opportunity, following the emperor's proposition, to advocate for his homeland, and request that which the princes had solicited of him. He recalled this but wavered in indecision…

"Prohaeresius is donning that plain cloak as though he has nothing to ask from this world," the proud sage replied.

After the emperor continued to insist, he went on:

"Athens, that city of wisdom, gave me intellectual nourishment. Everything I have, I owe to that city. I wished to advocate for Athens' physical nourishment."

He then portrayed the rampant poverty in the city, the high cost of food, which was increasing due to exorbitant tariffs, and finally, he requested that all the food entering the city—flour, wheat, and various provisions—be tariff-free.

Having lived in one of the poorest streets of Athens from a young age, the orator had very sad memories of the suffering of its citizens.

"Your request is very modest, but virtuous," the emperor said. "Let it be as you wish."

A command was written to the prefect Anatolius to lift the customs on food.

The orator then departed Rome for Athens. Arriving there, he fulfilled the Romans' request and sent one of his students, Eusebius of Alexandria, to impart lessons of wisdom and rhetoric in his place.

The two Armenian princes also accomplished their objective. Although Paruyr refused to spare one word to help them and considered it more fitting to advocate for the bread of the poor in Athens than to rescue all of Armenia from destruction, the magnanimous Armenian princes, scorning the xenomania of Armenia's degenerate son, were finally able to personally approach the emperor, and presenting him with the letter from St. Vrtanes and the Armenian lords, found him in willing agreement. The emperor fulfilled their request and went to Armenia with Antiochus' troops. Arriving, he reinstated peace, and Khosrov,[40] the son of Trdat, rose to the throne in his father's place.

Paruyr's advocation for lifting the tariffs increased his respect in the eyes of Athenians. They received him with great gratitude and returned his vacant rhetorician pulpit to him. He loved that pulpit more than an emperor loves his throne. From that pulpit, he ruled over minds, hearts, and spirits. He was dedicated to the pulpit from the depth of his soul. And it is not surprising, nor should he be blamed, for his indifference toward his homeland and its troubles. He was a lover of knowledge and wisdom. That love had caused him to forget all other loves.

He ruled Athens' rhetorical pulpit until the coronation of emperor Julian.[41] That persecutor

---

40 Khosrov III (330-339).
41 Julian the Apostate (361-363).

of Christianity and protector of pagan intellectuals, who distanced Christian scholars from all the schools and appointed pagans in their place—that apostate did not touch Paruyr; he left him in his place. Julian, who also considered him a great philosopher, had a profound reverence of Paruyr's knowledge and intelligence. He was personally acquainted with the orator and corresponded with him so much that he called him "Pericles' equal, the exuberant and unbounded master of eloquence" in one of his letters.

Julian also had a special expectation of the orator; he wished for Paruyr to write the history of his military exploits. He wished to immortalize his name through the masterful pen of the prominent orator. But the noble orator, who was not accustomed to engaging in flattery, refused his request, saying, "My hand does not record the history of the emperor who is a persecutor of Christ's instruction." After that refusal, the orator left the rhetorical pulpit of Athens of his own accord, wishing not to remain obliged to the emperor due to his position.

Among his many students, the most distinguished became the great Basil, who held the renowned Bishopric of Caesarea,[42] and St. Gregory

---

42 St. Basil of Caesarea (330-379).

the Theologian,[43] who with his voluminous works is eminent in Greek literature. To the latter's works belong Prohaeresius' epitaph placed at the head of this chapter. Also among his students was the young Eunapius, who wrote his dear teacher's biography.

As a man, Paruyr was not deprived of life's tender sides. When he was in the city of Tralles in Asia Minor, he fell in love with a Greek girl named Amphicleia, whom he married. From that marriage he had two daughters; after arranging their marriages to Greek husbands, he began to live separately from his wife, so as not to have his freedom impeded by familial affairs.

Paruyr lived deep into old age; he died at the age of 95. Virtue and unpretentiousness were the characteristics of his noble life, and solid and zealous work was the great strength of his indefatigable soul. He left behind a glorious name in Greek books. Athens boasted of him, and Rome erected a statue in his honor. Yet that great orator did not find even a small space in the heart of Armenians. None of our ancient manuscripts speak of him. He lived and worked for knowledge and wisdom, but was a lost man to his native land…

---

43 St. Gregory of Nazianzus (329-390).

It is true that he attained an eminent position among other great men of Greek history, but in that long line of names, his luster, intermixing with the radiance of many others, disappeared... If he had worked for his homeland, however, he would have been among the first—he would have been singular—and his memory would have been eternalized...

CHAPTER V

The blessed philosopher Movses [Khorenat-si], though still verily in the flesh, was already among the citizens of the heaven-ly host. Did the Armenian monks not, in fact, persecute him from place to place? Did they not, in their ignorance, call his illu-minating and ignorance-expelling writings "fraudulent"? And after turning hostile [to-ward him] in many other ways, on account of others' shame, they made the Saint drink the deadly poison of the false bishopric [...] They [the clerics] had his [Khorenatsi's] bones removed from his grave and thrown into the river. With the same restless perse-cution, they also put to death that angelic man Ter, and even now they still oppose the departed with the same spite!

–Ghazar Parpec'i

It was a stormy autumn night. The violent wind roared over the underground houses of the peasants and scattered the piles of grass that were heaped up on the roofs. The sky was cloudy and darkness ruled all around. Even the dogs had fled to their burrows that night and were waiting timidly, as though the end of the world was coming.

This was the village of Khorni in the province of Taron,[44] in which the oil lantern of one of the small huts was not yet put out. In one of the coves of that underground, subterranean dwelling, an elder was seated. The wind occasionally blew inside through an opening with a strong current and, causing the light of the lantern to waver, gave the elder's white-haired face mysterious expressions. He was alone. Surrounding him, on the same coarse rug on which he was seated, various old books in Greek, Iranian, and Syriac were scattered in a disorganized fashion. He was so engrossed in those old manuscripts that he did not so much as notice what was taking place outside. Those manuscripts were his intimate friends; they had been his faithful advisors since the day when, being persecuted from all sides, he began living a sad, solitary life in that pitiable hut.

The hut looked more like a tomb than the dwelling of a living man. It was that primitive form of dwelling from when humans did not differ much from wild beasts in their way of life. It was a perfect den. Even during the day, in order to see clearly, it was necessary to light a lantern. The musty, stale air was so heavy that it was suffocating. The walls were

---

44 Taron is a historic province of Armenia corresponding roughly to modern Muş in Turkey. Khorni is the village where Movses Khorenatsi (Moses of Khoren) is thought to have come from.

likewise covered with green mildew. The room was governed with dampness. Wherever you touched, the walls crumbled and soil would fall. Even the rocks were wearing away; they had disintegrated from the constant humidity. Yet the elderly scholar continued to live in that gloomy tomb—living at war with the ensnaring, decomposing, and enfeebling influence of his murderous environment.

He was happy in that dark tomb. He was happy in his state of bitter misfortune. Here, no one bothered him; here, he was forgotten, both by the world and by his numerous enemies. And that was enough for him to at least find the time to realize his lofty aim, before which all of life's afflictions had become immaterial and had left him in that dreadful state of self-denial. Poverty, hunger, and tribulation were inseparable from him; inseparable also were those manuscripts, with which he had surrounded himself, and in which he had found the only consolation of his heart.

The elder was Movses Khorenatsi. In the tribulations of that hut, he wrote his prodigious *History*, just as Israel's Moses, alone among the lightning and thunder atop Mount Sinai, wrote God's commandments on stone tablets.

The storm outside had not ceased, and the elder continued to pour words out onto the page. At that moment the melancholy creak of the hut door became audible. A young girl entered with delicate steps. Seeing the elder preoccupied, she wanted to depart just as quietly as she had entered. But the elder lifted his head, looked at her, and said:

"What is it, Shushanik?"

"I came to prepare your bed, Father."

"I am going to stay up. You go and sleep, my child."

Shushanik was the daughter of the elder's widowed sister. Her mother resided in the same hut, sharing in her brother's bitter poverty; she made tents and carpets, and supported her brother with her profits. Her daughter served him.

Despite the elder permitting her not to wait on him, but to go and rest, Shushanik started preparing his simple bed. On one side of the same coarse rug on which the elder was seated, she put down his pillow, which was filled with dry grass, and after spreading his blanket, which was made with coarse hair, she delicately approached her uncle to say goodnight according to her daily routine. The elder embraced her, and blessing her, kissed her goodnight. The fire of familial love had still not gone out in his broken heart. That graceful girl was as dear to him as his kind-hearted mother.

At that moment, the door of the hut started to intensely beat from outside.

"It must be the wind," the elder said.

"No, it is not the wind," Shushanik replied and ran outside to see who their untimely guest was.

A few minutes later she happily returned, saying:

"It's Husik, father."

"Husik?" the elder repeated in a surprised manner. "What is it? Why did he come?"

"He's wet; it's raining outside. He went to my mother to dry his clothes—he's coming to see you," Shushanik replied without paying attention to the elder's questions.

Husik was a young monk of the monastery of Saint Karapet,[45] and having been the elder's student as a child, he loved his teacher as though he was his own father. Although Husik's arrival made the elder boundlessly happy, he fell into a state of extreme distress when he considered what his unexpected arrival meant, having traveled through such a stormy and dangerous night to get there.

His distress grew worse when the young monk entered wearing secular clothes.

"What does this mean?" the elder proclaimed, terrified. "Why have you transformed? What misfortune has brought you here at this time of night, during such bad weather?"

---

45 Saint Karapet (John the Baptist) monastery (located near Muş in modern Turkey), now destroyed, is said to have been founded by St. Gregory the Illuminator in the 4th century.

"Relax, Father," the young monk replied, approaching the elder and receiving his blessing. "Nothing bad has happened. I will explain everything to you now."

He sat somewhat far from the elder. He explained that he had a sick brother in the neighboring village, and, requesting the abbot's permission, had come to see his brother—then, taking advantage of that occasion, he thought of visiting his teacher as well. And his reason for coming by night and changing his clothes, which should have been evident to his teacher, was that the other monks looked upon the elder's visitors with suspicion.

In truth, the first part of his story was completely fabricated; he neither had a sick brother, nor was he going to visit him. He had actually come straight to the elder, but with what objective? He carefully kept silent about that, not wishing to agitate his already broken heart.

The elder relaxed a little.

"Yes, it is apparent to me," he said with particular bitterness, "that the Armenian monks look upon my visitors with suspicion, considering them sectarians…" then he changed the topic. "Tell me what news there is from your monastery."

The young man started to tell him about the various monastic intrigues, about the laziness of the monks and the extortion that took place there.

The elder listened uninterestedly, as though it were a customary thing, and with his head hanging, and without looking at the young man's face, he carefully collected the books scattered around him and put them off to one side. He collected them all except for one that he had written and kept it in his hand. That book was familiar to the young man, who asked interestedly:

"You have not finished yet, father?"

"The *History* is complete. Today I wrote my lament—that is, the conclusion of my work."

"Where does the *History* conclude?"

"With the Arsacid dynasty and the fall of the Patriarchal Chair of the line of our Illuminating father.[46] I could not go further and portray the disgraceful acts of our current monks. You are aware how infuriated they are with me even without that."

The young man took the book from the elder's hand and began leafing through the pages, reading only the chapter headings.

"This much is sufficient," he said with particular satisfaction.

"In that book I have summarized the acts of our predecessors, both good and bad; I have portrayed the evildoings of the traitors of our land and

---

46 The patriarchal chair of Armenia refers to the Catholicosate, of which the founding father was St Gregory the Illuminator.

the self-sacrifice of our patriots. It is a testament that I am leaving to the future generation. These centuries of darkness and ignorance will pass, and an age of light will be born with its new children. Those children will see in this testament both the beautiful and ugly memories of our past. They will start to examine and judge the works of their fore-fathers, and learning from the mistakes of the past and taking joy from the good examples, they will create a new life on firmer, safer foundations. They will reap the benefit of the trials of the past and will work to avoid falling into the abyss of loss, where their forefathers mindlessly fell…"

"And your name will be immortalized for leaving to the future such a mirror, in which the coming generation will see the sad memories of the past. It will see its former greatness as well as its painful downfall…" the young man interrupted the elder's speech.

"I do not think at all about immortality," the elder replied with sincere modesty. "I have worked to immortalize the memories of our homeland, so that they do not perish and are not forgotten in the minds of our people. Nothing is so painful as a people who do not know the history of their predecessors. That misfortune is one and the same as a father passing away without leaving anything written behind for his young heirs.

The young monk was listening carefully; his intelligent face expressed a particular discomfort. It was as though he was quietly saying to himself, 'That is all very beautiful and very instructive, but we still have a long time to talk about that; now it is necessary to discuss a most important issue.'

"Do you not intend to change your dwelling, father?" he said, unable to wait any longer.

"What do you mean?" the elder asked with unease.

"Nothing… I'm just asking…"

"So they wish to expel me from here too?"

"No… but… it wouldn't be bad to take some precaution…"

"Where shall I move to? Where shall I go?" the elder replied in a bitter manner. "There was a time when my powers were not depleted; there was a gleam in my eye and strength in my feet. I drifted from one side of our land to the other, withstood hunger, thirst, and the austerities of the seasons. And now, where am I to go? Where can I drag this broken machine?" He brought his hand closer to himself. "My life passed with pains and bitterness; there hasn't remained one torment that I haven't borne. And now, how can they deprive me of this one last consolation, without letting me spend the last days of my old age in this damp tomb?"

He gestured to his dwelling, and following a momentary silence continued more bitterly:

"I left, I went away from them, and started searching for my heart's comfort in solitude. I left them behind to their rich monasteries and the profiteering bishops of their provinces. Let them enjoy that; let them accumulate gold and silver, because worldly pleasures are sweet for them. I do not bother them, and as much as I wished to do so, I would have been unable to because they have the power of other nakharars on their side and the protection of foreigners, which they receive at the expense of their homeland. What do they want from me now? They gave me the bishopric of Bagrevand only to mock me, to lift me up, and then knock me down from that higher place, so that my downfall would be more palpable. I withstood all of that, I endured every deprivation. My fight was not for glory. I was at war with darkness, ignorance, and the traitors of our homeland. I was vanquished, I fell, and my glory is in my downfall. Why don't they leave me to repose in my ruins now? I took refuge in my poor hut in my homeland. Behold, all my wealth." He gestured his hand toward the manuscripts beside him. "I became deprived of the world and of my community, and now they want to prevent me from consulting and consoling myself with those silent, mute manuscripts in my moments of misfortune? They seized everything from me—only a pen remained. Are they going to seize that too, so that I am unable to express my thoughts, the bitter feelings of my heart?"

The oppressed truth of time was speaking through the afflicted elder's mouth.

"There is even more wickedness you need to beware of…" the young monk replied in an affected manner. "Those darkness-lovers have no limit to the oppression they inflict. They constantly seek new opportunities to beat you down. And the final blow will be catastrophic…"

"Are they thinking of poisoning me according to their old custom?" the old man asked with bitter scorn. "I do not fear poison."

"It is true, you do not fear it; they have tried that a few times with you. But…"

"What else can they do now except murder me? There cannot be a worse condition that they could subject me to. Let them expel me from this pitiable hut. Even in the cavities of the mountains and rocks, I will find a cave to shelter in. Our Patriarch, the Illuminator, died in such a cave following his persecution by the ignorance of those darkness-lovers. And I am not even worthy of being his modest student."

"If that were the extent of vengefulness of the persecutors, we could have been satisfied. But their intentions are even more evil than that…"

"Tell me then, at last. Torment me. What do they wish to do?"

"They are thinking of stealing all your literary works and destroying them. They are thinking of exterminating your *History* that is the fruit of the heavy labor of your final years. In order to deliver this painful news to you, I secretly left the monastery and hurried to you to forewarn you."

"Criminals!" exclaimed the old man exclaimed anxiously. "I expected every lowliness from them, but even I could not imagine that. That is a tremendous crime—to kill history! That is the greatest of all faults. Do they also wish to destroy our previous works and bury our history into eternal oblivion so that their evil deeds are concealed, forgotten, and do not become a subject of shame and censure in the future? Yes, that would be a fatal blow for me, if they achieved that objective. This manuscript remained my final consolation; I condensed my heart, my spirit, and all my feelings into it. I put my tears into it, which I had spilled upon the ruins of our homeland…

He left his head bowed and raised his hand toward his forehead. The elder's white hair spilled over his venerable face and covered his tears, which flowed from his eyes like a flood. He remained in that saddened condition for several minutes. Then he continued in a more furious manner:

"The unfortunate consequences of those circumstances do not grieve me. The battle between the light and darkness of our time could not have finished in such a manner. The first students of our fathers Sahak and Mesrop were in the first class of warriors. They have fallen. The younger students—myself and my friends—were in the second class. We passed over the corpses of our predecessors; though we got quite far, we too fell. Our strengths were disproportionate. We needed to uproot the ignorance and prejudices that had sprouted and flourished for centuries; we needed to clean the moral filth that had accumulated and condensed over the centuries in the people's hearts. This was not an easy task. We needed to fall like our predecessors. Some generations needed to be sacrificed, until a path emerged over their corpses toward light, toward truth, and toward goodness. My friends are now subject to the same persecution as me. We are not thinking of ourselves. But what will be sorrowful is if our enemies succeed at obliterating our works, the fruits of our labors…"

"Perhaps it is not hopeless; perhaps there are ways to save your literary works," the young monk replied with a certain assurance. "You have written your *History* at the request of your patron, Sahak Bagratuni. You intended to personally take your work and dedicate it to the noble prince with your own hands. Your enemies have understood that. They are prepared to seize that invaluable treasure, either from your home or on your travels. We cannot lose time. If my gracious teacher has faith in his devoted student, I am prepared to take the journey tonight to deliver your book to the prince. After it reaches his hands, your work will be rescued from danger.

The elder embraced his dear student and praised him, saying:

"You have always been gracious and inclined toward the truth and that which is good, Husik. I praise your devotion and am solaced, because you yourself are one of the fruits of my labor. If there were many like you, our hopes would have been crowned. We accomplished our work, we tilled our soil, and we sowed our crop. Hereafter, it remains to you to cultivate the land and to nourish the nascent sprouts, so that the thorns and thistles do not suffocate them. Hereafter, you and those like you need to continue the work we started. I bless you and pray for your firm will, fervor, and strength from the Almighty. Take that manuscript and deliver it to the prince. He is the only one who knows to value it, he is the only one who venerates the recollections of his predecessors; he is the only one who has suffered these miseries with me. The Bagratunis have always been loyal to the origins of the Armenians' profits. He will preserve the book as a relic and transmit it to his descendants. I see through the eyes of my soul that the princely scepter of the Armenians will one day dawn again from the Bagratuni line. And that line, which used to crown the Armenian kings, will come to crown itself. Impart my prophecy to the prince."

The book was placed in a leather sack; the young monk tied it around his waist and wore his cloak on top. Then he took his traveling staff and, kissing the elder's right hand, departed.

The storm outside was still raging, the rain was pouring as in a torrent, and the violent wind was moving the craggy rocks from their places, but the courageous traveler made his way with a bold step to Sahak Bagratuni's fortress, which was a several days' journey from Khorenatsi's village.

—

The chiming… the untimely chiming of the bells… which inflicts terror! The heavy, sorrowful ringing of the bells was audible from all sides. It was audible from the small bell tower of the village, from the high bell towers of the monasteries, from the solitary, isolated chapels in remote valleys and uninhabited mountains. Everywhere, the heartless metal was ringing. It was ringing with its ominous sound of invitation.

It was not the same sound that invites the devout villagers to God's temple to offer their doxology of gratitude to the Almighty. It was a sound that gave rise to dread, that foreshadowed some disaster, some alarm, some misfortune, that portends danger.

The day was just dawning. The sky was peaceful, and the sun's bright rays were smiling on the dewy foliage. Nature was rejoicing in her astonishing beauty—it appeared as though she did not hear the dreadful sound of the bells and was not troubled by it.

But the people were in a great disturbance. Everyone was running out of their dwellings to see what had happened. The monks in black ran out in groups; some with cowls, some without; some not finding time to wear their slippers. The ominous sound reached as far as the solitary cell of the ascetic in the mountainous cave, and he too left his dark enclosure.

The villagers had just started working the fields. The harvester left his harvest, departing with his sickle in hand. The farmer left his plow with his whip in hand. The peaceful villagers poured out of their settlements with their spades and pickaxes. Wives, carrying their children, followed their husbands.

Where were they hurrying to? They themselves did not know. The bells were ringing. The sound of the church was calling them.

Somewhere, an indeterminate darkness resembling an obscure mass was perceptible. The villagers were making their way toward it. The mass appeared small from afar, but as they approached it, it was growing, expanding, and taking the form of a crowd of people.

From all sides, they were going toward that center. There was a drunken state in the crowd, where their wild instincts reached monstrous fervor, and they no longer accounted for themselves, but, like a furious torrent, poured forth, wreaked destruction in brutish cruelty, and annihilated everything that happened along their path. The commoner's fury takes on a more terrifying character when he is led by the clergy—when religious fanaticism mixes with his work. When this happens, fury is consecrated in the name of the church and God. The same fanaticism created the shameful hanging and multiplied the number of auto-da-fés.

Here too an auto-da-fé was being performed. But they were not burning people alive; rather, inanimate objects.

A fire was burning in the public square. The clergy were surrounding it. A great smoke was rising from the woodpile and, diffusing and surrounding the monks in black like a dark cloud, gave the characteristic appearance that a black deed was about to be performed.

Books were piled on one side of the fire. One of the monks read the anathema then took one of the books and threw it on top of the woodpile. The others followed his example. The manuscripts, like a sacrificial offering, began to flicker and burn. And a great man's age-old works turned to ashes within a few minutes…

The commoners' cries of joy intensified in the air. From every mouth was heard: "We're saved from the books of the sectarians… there will no longer be pain, plague, and drought in our land…"

The superstition of the commoners and persecution by the monks did not end at that. There remained one more source of pain, plague, drought, and various other scourges. That too needed to be destroyed.

The crowd of commoners started moving to one side. Nothing was comprehensible in the confusion of all the noise and clamoring. A kind of wild, morbid spirit ruled over them all. They surrounded an unadorned tomb that was encircled by thickets. One of the monks led by example; he took his pickaxe and started digging. Numerous others with spades and pickaxes followed. In a few minutes the tomb was opened. They filled sacks with the remains of the "sectarian's" body. The women transported the soil from the grave in their aprons and the flaps of their clothes with particular fervency. They cleaned out everything; they took everything. Not even a trace of the tomb remained. Then, with cries of exultation, the celebratory procession went toward the nearby river. They threw the "sectarian's" bones and dirt from his grave into the water. The waves rippled, the river continued its peaceful flow, and the victim of the clergy's persecution was covered beneath the icy billows…

These were the remains of Movses Khorenatsi's body.

At that same moment, when this shameful act was being conducted, a young monk, standing alone upon an elevation, was watching from afar. He was anger incarnate; he watched with deep agitation, and the following words flew out of his trembling lips:

"Children of darkness… You persecuted the laborious cultivator of our newborn literature for his entire life. His old age passed with pain and bitterness. Only in his grave was he to find rest—and you deprived him even of that peace… Future generations will seal your conduct with curses and anathemas… And he, whose memory you worked to erase from the face of the earth—he will be immortal forever in the heart of every Armenian…"

That dissenter was Khorenatsi's student Husik.[47]

---

47 In writing *Prohaeresius*, we took poetic license with a small anachronism to bring the times of Paruyr and Khorenatsi closer to each other, though they were not too far apart. And the facts of history we tried to defend, so much as is pardonable in fiction.

Պ ԱՐՈՅՐ
ՀԱՅԿԱՁՆ

(ՊՐՈՅԵՐԵՍԻՈՍ)

ԳԼՈՒԽ Ա

որրորդ դարում, երբ Հայաստանից շատ մանուկներ դիմում էին Աթէնք ուսում առնելու, այդ քաղաքի յետ ընկած փողոցներից մէկում, փոքրիկ խրճիթի մէջ, ապրում էր մի երիտասարդ: Նա բնակվում էր խրճիթի ստորին ամենաանշուք սենեակներից մէկում, ուր օդի եւ լոյսի պակասութիւնը տալիս էր նրան գերեզմանի նմանութիւն: Ոչինչ կարասիք չկար այդ գետնափոր նկուղի մէջ, յարդով ծածկված էր նրա խոնաւ յատակը եւ մի քանի հնամաշ կապերտներ ծառայում էին եւ որպէս անկողին, եւ որպէս սփռոց: Պատուհաններում երեւում էին մագաղաթեայ գրչագրներ, կաշեայ հաստ կազմերով:

Սենեակը նեղ էր: Նրա անձկութիւնը աւելի անտանելի էր դառնում, որովհետեւ երիտասարդը մի ընկեր եւս ունէր: Նրան կոչում էին Հեփեստիօն, իսկ ինքը կոչվում էր Պրոյերեսիոս:

Քաղաքի այն թաղը, ուր կենում էին երկու երիտասարդները, բնակեցրած էր այնպիսի աղքատ ժողովրդով, որոնք միայն օրեկան աշխատանքի, օրեկան հացի համար են մտածում, այդ պատճառով նրանց շատ չէր հետաքրքրում երիտասարդների մտաւոր պարապմունքը, եւ չգիտէին անգամ, թէ դրանք ինչով էին պարապում:

Միայն իրանց արտաքին կերպարանքով երիտասարդները գրաւում էին հարեւանների ուշադրութիւնը։ Պրոյերեսիոսը ուժեղ էր, վայելչակազմ եւ դեմքով գեղեցիկ։ Նրա կենսագրութիւնը մեզ աւանդող Եւնաբիոսը ասում է, որ ուքն ուոք բարձրութիւն ունէր եւ իր ժամանակի ամենաբարձրահասակ տղամարդերի մօտ, դարձեալ կարող էր իբրեւ հսկայ ներկայանալ։ Որի ընդհակառակն, Հեփեստիօնը միջակ հասակ ունէր, գունաթափ եւ հիւանդոտ դեմք։

Երկու երիտասարդները այն աստիճան սիրում էին միմեանց, որ նրանց մէջ բնակվում էր մէկ սիրտ, մէկ հոգի եւ մէկ կամք։ Չնայելով, որ նրանք երկու միմեանց հակառակ ազգութիւնների էին պատկանում, բայց գիտութեան զաղափարը եղբայրացրել էր նրանց։ Պրոյերեսիոսը հայ էր, իսկ Հեփեստիօնը՝ յոյն։ Երկուսն էլ ուսանողներ էին։

Պրոյերեսիոսի հայկական անունը Պարոյր էր. եւ եւ այս անունով պիտի կոչեմ նրան։

Հոգով միացած լինելով, երկու ուսանողները միասին բաժանում էին եւ իրանց դառն աղքատութիւնը։ Բացի մի վերարկուից եւ պատմուճանից, երկուսն էլ դրսում հագնելու համար ուրիշ հագուստ չունէին։ Այդ վերարկուն եւ պատմուճանը հերթով հագնում էին նրանք, երբ մէկը գնում էր դասախօսութիւն լսելու, իսկ միւսը ստիպված էր տանը մնալ։ Հարեւանների

ծիծաղին չափ չը կար, երբ ճերթը Հեփեստի-
ունին էր հասնում, երբ փոքրիկ Հեփեստիօնը,
կուլուված բարձրահասակ Պարոյրի վերարկուի
եւ պատմուճանի մէջ, շտապում էր դէպի ճեմա-
րան:

Տանտիրուհին, որը մի բարի արհեստա-
ւորի կին էր, շատ գոհ չէր երիտասարդ ուսա-
նողներից: Այդ դժգոհութիւնը առաջ էր գալիս
ոչ թէ այն պատճառից, որ նրանք ամիսներով
իրանց բնակարանի վարձը վճարել չէին կարողանում,—այլ առաւելապէս նրանից, որ շատ
անգամ, գիշերները, նրանց ստորերկրեայ նկուղից լսելի էին լինում օտարոտի ձայներ, որպէս
թէ մէկը ոգեւորուած, բորբոքուած ճառախօսում
է, իսկ միւսը նրան նոյնքան բորբոքուած կերպով
նկատողութիւններ է անում, կամ հարցեր է առա-
ջարկում: Ճառախօսութիւնները երբեմն տեւում
էին ամբողջ գիշերներ, եւ միւշեւ լոյս անբնդ-
հատ կերպով թնդեցնում էին մթին նկուղի ան-
ձուկ մթնոլորտը: Սնահաւատ տան տիրուհին
նրանց խելագարների տեղ էր դնում, կարծում
էր, թէ ոգիների հետ են խօսում եւ միշտ տրտնջում էր, թէ իր երեխաները վախենում են, եւ
քնել չեն կարողանում: Երիտասարդները թէեւ
խոստանում էին, որ այլեւս ձայն չեն բարձրացնի,
բայց իրանց խոստմունքը կատարել չէին կարողանում: Ոգեւորութիւնը անգապելի է: Նրանք
ճարտասանական մարզութիւնների ժամանակ

միշտ մոռանում էին իրանց շրջապատը:

Այսպես, պատերազմելով կեանքի եւ աղքատութեան հետ, երիտասարդ ուսանողները մի քանի տարիներ անցկացրին փիլիսոփայութեան եւ ճարտասանութեան մայրաքաղաքում, մինչեւ Պարոյրը իր զարմանալի յառաջադիմութեամբ գրաւեց իր վարժապետի, կապադովկացի Յուլիանոսի, ուշադրութիւնը, որը տեսնում էր իր աշակերտի մէջ խիստ փայլուն ապագայ:

Երբ Յուլիանոսը Աթէնքից հեռացաւ, շատերը աշխատում էին նրա ամբիոնը ժառանգել: Առաջարկվեցան հինգ ընտրելիներ:[1] Մրցութիւնը սաստիկ էր. Աթէնքը մի քանի կուսակցութիւն-ների էր բաժանված եւ իւրաքանչիւր կողմը աշ-խատում էր իր կանդիդատի ընտրութիւնը յա-ջողեցնել: Ամենավատն այն էր, որ այդ ժամա-նակ Հռոմէական կառավարութիւնը մտցրել էր գիտութեան ազատ տաճարի մէջ իր ճանշոդ եւ ամեն յառաջադիմութիւն ոչնչացնող ձեռքը: Այդ պատճառով աւելի շուտ ընդունելութիւն էին գտ-նում ոչ թէ ճշմարիտ գիտնականները, այլ քսու-ները, կեղծաւորները, որոնք շողոքորթում էին կառավարութեան հաճոյքները: Այդ կետից նա-յելով, արդարամիտ եւ անկաշառելի Պարոյրի ընտրութիւնը բոլորովին անյուսալի էր:

<hr>

1 Պարոյրը, նրա ընկեր Հեփեստիոնը, եպիփանոսը, Դիոփան-տեը, Սոպոլիտէը եւ Պառնասիոսը:

Բայց Պարոյրը կայսրութեան զաւառներում եւ նահանգներում մեծ հռչակ ունէր: Եւ որովհետեւ նահանգներից եւս բազմաթիւ մանուկներ էին ուղարկում Աթէնք ուսանելու, այդ պատճառով նահանգներն եւս ճայնի իրաւունք ունէին: Արեւելքի մեծ մասը ընտրում էր Եպիփանոսին, Արաբիան՝ Դիովանտէսին, իսկ Պարոյրի համար ճայն էին տալիս բոլոր Պոնտացիք եւ Բիւթանիա, Հելլեսպոնտոս եւ Ասիայի այն մասը, որ Կարիայէն տարածվում է մինչեւ Լիդիա, Պամֆիլիա եւ Տաւրոսի լեռները: Այդ կողմերում Պարոյրը ընդարձակ ժողովրդականութիւն ունէր: Հեփեստիոնը իր ընկերի հետ մրցութիւն անել չկամեցաւ, նա ասպարէզը թողեց Պարոյրին եւ ինքը հեռացաւ Աթէնքից: Պարոյրի ընտրութիւնը յաջողվեցաւ, եւ Հայկազն հռետորը, իր տոկուն աշխատութեամբ, մթին նկուղից բարձրացաւ Աթէնքի փիլիսոփայութեան եւ ճարտասանութեան ճեմարանի ամբիոնը:

Մեր հռետորը իր փառքի հետ ժառանգեց եւ բազմաթիւ նախանձորդներ: Նրա թշնամի հռետորները ամենաանվայել հնարներով աշխատում էին վնասել նրան: Պարոյրի զօրաւոր հանճարը եւ երկաթի հաստատամտութիւնը միայն կարող էր երկար ընդդիմադրել նրանց ցած դաւադրութիւններին: Բայց վերջը հակառակութիւնը այն աստիճան հասաւ, որ նրան զրպարտեցին քաղաքական հանցանքների մէջ, եւ տեղային հռոմէական նահանգապետի հրամանով Պարոյրը աքսորվեցաւ Աթէնքից։

Աքսորանքի դառնութեան հետ նա նորից սկսեց կրել աղքատութեան դառնութիւնը։ Բայց այդ վերջինին վաղուց ընտելացած էր նա։ Նրան տանջում էր միայն անգործութեան տաղտկութիւնը։ Նրան աքսորել էին Յունիական ծովի համարեա անբնակ կղզիներից մէկի մէջ։

Երկար Պարոյրը աքսորանքի մէջ նեղութիւններ էր կրում, մինչեւ Աթէնքի նահանգապետը փոխվեցաւ եւ նրա տեղը նորը նշանակվեցաւ։ Այդ ժամանակ հռետորի բարեկամները աշխատեցին աքսորանքից նրան վերադարձնելու, որ եւ կարողացան յաջողացնել։

Պարոյրը Աթէնք վերադառնալով, իր բարեկամներից շատերին վախճանված գտաւ։ Նրա զգայուն սրտին մեծ ցաւ պատճառեց նրանցից երկուսի մահը. մէկը՝ նրա ընկեր Հեփեստիօնն էր, միւսը՝ նրա բարեկամ Տուսկիանոսը։ Վերջինի կենսագրութիւնը գրող Սուտիասը «ամենագոր ճարտասան» է անուանում հանգուցեալին. իսկ մեր հայկազն հռետորի կենսագրութիւնը մեզ աւանդող Եւնաբիոսը ասում է՝ թէ «Նա (Տուսկիանոսը) միայն արժան էր Պրոյերեսիոս լինելու, եթէ Պրոյերեսիոսը ողջ չլիներ...»։

Պարոյրը Աթէնք գնալուց յետոյ, նրա թշնամիները նորից գրգռվեցան, նորից սկսեցին

նրա դէմ որոգայթներ լարել: Նոր նահանգա֊
պետը ստիպվեցաւ հրապարակական հանդիսա֊
ւոր ատեան կազմել եւ Պարոյրին իր հակառա֊
կորդների հետ մրցութեան հրաւիրել: Հանդի֊
սականները հաւաքված էին եւ հակառակ կող֊
մերը ներկայ էին: Մի կողմում Պարոյրը, միւս
կողմում մի խումբ հռետորներ: Մրցութեան տե֊
ման պետք է տար ինքը նահանգապետը, իսկ
նրանք յանպատրաստից պետք է ճառախօսէին:
Պարոյրի ախոյանները հրաժարվեցան, յայտնե֊
լով, թէ իրանք առանց նախապատրաստութեան
բան չեն խօսի: Այդ ժամանակ նահանգապետը
դիմեց դէպի հայկազն հռետորը, որը աներկիւղ
ամբիոն բարձրացաւ եւ առաջարկեց, որ իր հա֊
կառակորդները ինչ տեմա որ ցանկանում են
թող տան: Նրանք էլ չարամտութեամբ մի այն֊
պիսի տեմա տուեցին, որ ոչ միայն անյարմար
էր պերճախօսութեան, այլ գրեթէ անհնարին էր
յանպատրաստից նրա վրա մի բան խօսել:

Բայց մեր հռետորը չր վհատեցաւ, նա մի֊
այն խնդրեց նշանագրողներին արձանագրել իր
ասածները, որ վերջը վիճաբանութեան տեղիք
չմնայ, թէ ինքը բոլոր կէտերին չէ պատասխա֊
նել, եւ խնդրեց հասարակութեանը, որ ծափա֊
հարութիւններով չր խանգարեն իրան:

Ատենախօսութիւնը այն աստիճան սքան֊
չելի եւ իմաստալից եղաւ, որ ունկնդիրները, յա֊
փշտակված նրա ազդու պերճախօսութիւնից,

բոլորովին մոռացան իրանց խոսումունքը, եւ ոգեւորված բացականչութիւններով ու ծափահարութեամբ թնդեցնում էին ամֆիթէատրոնի կամարները:

Նշանագրողները հազիւ կարողանում էին հասցնել նրա խոսքերի հոսանքի եւեւից, որոնք առատաբուխ վտակի նման վազում էին նրա շրթունքներից: Երբ վերջացրեց, հանդիսականները աւելի ոգեւորված կեցցէներով բազմիցս ողջունում էին նրան:

Բայց Պարոյրը իր զարմանալի սրամտութեան զօրութիւնը ցոյց տալու համար, խնդրեց հանդիսականներից, որ նորից կրկնէ իր ճառը, որպէս զի նշանագրողները համեմատեն իրանց գրուածի հետ, մի գուցէ մի բան թողած լինի: Եւ նա սկսեց ամբողջ ճառը առաջին բառից մինչեւ վերջին բառը անփոփոխ նորից ասել: Նշանագրողները ոչինչ տարբերութիւն չգտան, կարծես թէ, շատ առաջուց սերտած լինէր այն բոլորը, ինչ որ հանպատրաստից խոսեց նա:

Պարոյրը տարաւ մրցանակը: Բազմութիւնը խնդակցութեամբ սեղմեց նրա ձեռքը, անուանելով նրան Հերմէս — պերճախոսութեան աստուած: Նահանգապետը իր սեպհական կառքով, զինուորական երամշտութեամբ, եւ հանդիսաւոր փառքով տարաւ նրան մինչեւ բնակարանը:

Հայկազն հռետորը իր փառքի օրերը անց էր կացնում միեւնոյն բնակարանում, ուր անցու

ցել էր իր ուսանողական կեանքի դառն աղքատութիւնը: Առաջին եւ այժմեան կեցութեան մէջ
այն զանազանութիւնը կար միայն, որ Աթէնքի
պերճախօսութեան աստուածը փոխանակ նոյն
խրճթի ստորին նկուղի մէջ ապրելու, այժմ կենում էր նրա վերին յարկում, մի փոքրիկ սենեակի
մէջ: Ապրուստի եղանակը մնացել էր նոյնը.—
նոյն սպարտական խստակեցութիւնը, նոյն չա-
փաւորութիւնը իր ամենապարզ վայելքներով
թագաւորում էր նրա անշուք բնակարանի մէջ:
Պատմական վերարկուն եւ պատմուճանը, որը
երբեմն հագնում էր ինքը եւ երբեմն նրա սիրելի
ընկեր Հեփեստիօնը, պահվում էր այդ բնակարանում որպէս մի թանգազին յիշատակ ուսանողական եղբայրութեան եռանդոտ եւ ամեն
զոհողութիւնների համբերող կեանքի: Այժմ նրա
միամիտ տան տիրուհին այլեւս դժգոհ չէր, այլեւս չէր տրտնջում, բայց մի առանձին հպարտու-
թեամբ պարծենում էր իր հարեւանների մօտ, որ
իր տանը կենում է մի մեծ մարդ:

Նոյն օրը, երբ Աթէնքի այդ աղքատ թաղի
փողոցները որոտում էին բազմութեան կեցցէներով, երբ Պարոյրին յաղթական փառքով տանում
էին դէպի իր բնակարանը, ամբոխի մէջ գտնվում
էր եւ մի անձանօթ օտարական: Նա բոլորովին
աննկատելի մնաց խուռն բազմութեան մէջ, թէեւ
նրա դէմքը, օտարոտի հագուստը բաւական աչքի
ընկնող էր:

Օրը անցավ, մութը պատեց, աղքատ թաղի փողոցները դատարկվեցան մարդիկներից։ Բայց օտարականը միայնակ դեռ թափառում էր այնտեղ։ Նա մի քանի անգամ մօտեցաւ այն խրճիթին, ուր բնակվում էր օրվայ հերոսը։ Բայց նկատելով, որ դեռ նրա մօտ մարդիկ կան, ներս չմտաւ։

Նա շարունակեց ման գալ, մինչեւ մարդիկը դուրս կը գային։ Հարիւր անգամ անցուդարձ արեց փողոցի երկարութեամբ եւ ամեն անգամ մօտենում էր դռանը, ականջը դնում էր նրա ճեղքին, եւ դարձեալ ճայներ էր լսում։ Օրը սկսել էր լուսանալ․ զիղացինները աւանակներով նապարներ էին տանում դէպի հրապարակը․ այդ մարդը դեռ այն փողոցից չէր հեռացել։

Հետեւեալ օրուայ միջօրէի պահուն, մի նոր բազմութիւն ուրախաձայն աղաղակներով, դարձեալ դիմում էր դէպի հռետորի բնակարանը։ Օտարականը խառնվեցաւ այդ բազմութեան հետ։—Էլ ի՞նչ կայ,—հարցրեց նա մէկից։—Կայսրի հրովարտակն են տանում,—պատասխանեց նա։

Մի փառք միւս փառքի ետեւից։ Կոստանդ կայսրը կոչում էր հռետորին իր մօտ։

Օտարականը այդ լսելով, գլուխը շարժեց եւ հեռացաւ։

ԳԼՈՒԽ Բ

Երկու օր անցել էր, երբ մի գիշեր օտարականը դարձեալ յայտնվեցաւ հյուրանոցի խարճիթի դռանը: Ներսից ձայն չէր լսվում: Նա սկսեց բաղխել դուռը: Սպասաւորը պատասխանեց, թէ իր տերը շատ յոգնած է, թէ այս մի քանի գիշեր է, որ նա ամենեւին չէ քնել. մարդիկ նրան հանգստութիւն չէին տալիս, այժմ պատրաստվում է հանգստանալ, եւ հրամայել է ոչ ոքին չընդունել:

—Ասա՛ քո տիրոջը, որ ես նրա հայրենիքիցն եմ եւ կ'ըndունէ ինձ,—խոսեց օտարականը:

Մի րոպէից յետոյ դուռը բացվեցաւ եւ օտարականը ներս հրաւիրվեցաւ: Հռետորը առանց ճանաչելու նրան, առանց հարցնելու թէ ով է, միայն հայաստանցի լինելը լսելով, հենց իր սենեակի շեմքի վրա գրկախառնեց նրա հետ:

Օտարականը մի երիտասարդ էր բաւական բարձրահասակ, եւ ամուր կազմված. երկար ժամանակ Եգիպտոսի արեգակի տակ գտնվելով, նրա պայծառ դէմքը ստացել էր պղնձի ախորժելի գոյն: Երկայն գիսակները խիտ գանգուրներով իջել էին մինչեւ նրա ուսերը, իսկ գլուխը փաթաթած էր ծաղկաւոր ապարոշով, որի ծայրերը անփոյթ կերպով ձգած լին նրա լայն թիկունքի վրա: Սեւորակ աչքերի մէջ նրշ-մարվում էր խորին տխրութիւն, որ արտափայլում էր ամբողջ դէմքի վրա: Այդ թախծալի

տրտմութիւնը իսկոյն նկատեց հիւտտորը, մանաւանդ երբ նա լուռ, առանց մի բառ խոսելու,
կանցաւ եւ նստեց բազմոցի վրա:

Այդ ի՞նչ էր նշանակում: Այդ քանի օր էր,
որ ամէն օք խնդակցութեամբ էր հանդիպում
նրան, ամէն օք արտայայտում էր իր ջերմ
ուրախութիւնը նրա յաջողութեան համար, իսկ
նրա հայրենակիցը մի բառ անգամ չարտասանեց այդ մասին, որպէս թէ ոչինչ չէր տեսել, ոչինչ չգիտէր: Նրա առաջին խոսքը այս եղաւ.

—Այստեղ մեզ չե՞ն խանգարի:

—Ի՞նչու համար էք հարցնում,—ասաց հրռետորը:

—Ես առանձին խոսելիք ունեմ ձեզ հետ:

—Բայց նախ եւ առաջ պէտք է գիտենամ, թէ
դուք ո՞վ էք:

Օտարականը ծանոթություն տուեց իր մասին:

—Ես ձեր մասին լսել եմ... բացականչեց
հիւտտորը, եւ ուրախութեամբ մօտենալով, կրկին
անգամ գրկախառնվեցաւ նրա հետ:

Երբ միամտացալ օտարականը, որ իրանք
միայնակ են, տանեցիք բոլորը քնած են, եւ մանաւանդ իրանց խոսակցութեան լեզուն այստեղ
ոչ օք հասկանալ կարող չէր, ասաց.

—Գիշերի կէսից անցել է. ժամանակ չկորցնենք, խոսենք, ինչ որ պէտք է խոսքինք. ես երկար այստեղ մնալու չեմ, առաւօտեան պէտք է ճանապարհ ընկնեմ:

—Այժմ ո՞րտեղից էք գալիս:

—Հռոմից: Եգիպտոսից այնտեղ գնացի, յետոյ այստեղ եկայ առ ժամանակ մնալու դի-տաւորութեամբ, բայց հանգամանքները փոխվե-ցան... այլեւս մնալ չեմ կարող...

—Ի՞նչու:

—Հայրենիքից վատ լուրեր ստացայ. շտա-պում եմ այնտեղ:—Վերջին խօսքերը այնպիսի մի դառնութեամբ արտասանեց նա, որ Պարոյրի մէջ եւս տխրութիւն ազդեց:

—Արտասուն՛քի եւ արեան աշխա՛րհ,—բա-ցականչեց նա,—ե՞րբ է եղել, որ մի մխիթարական լուր լսենք այնտեղից:

Այժմ հանգամանքները աւելի վատացել են, —խոսեց երիտասարդը,—Վռամշապուհը, հայոց աշխարհի լուսաւորութեան ջահը իր հզոր ձեռ-քով առաջ տանող թագաւորը, վաղուց արդէն վախճանված է: Նրանից յետոյ Արշակունեաց ջահը փոքր ժամանակներով ժառանգեցին մի քանի աննշան թագաւորներ, մինչեւ աւելի ա-նարժանը, երիտասարդ Արտաշիրը թագաւոր դարձաւ: Առաջ դժբախտութիւնը միշտ դրսից էր գալիս, բայց դրա ժամանակ սկսեց ներսից ծագել: Երիտասարդ թագաւորը իր թեթեւամիտ վարքով գրգռեց իր դէմ հայոց նախարարների զզուանքը, որոնք աւելի եւս անմիտ գտնվելով, դիմեցին պարսից Վռամ արքային, խնդրելով, որ Արտաշիրին գահընկեց անէ եւ նրա տեղը մի պարսիկ մարզպան դնէ Հայաստանը կառավարելու համար: Պարսից արքայի վաղուց փափագած բաղձանքը հէնց այս էր, նա ամենայն սիրով կատարեց նախարարների ցանկութիւնը: Մեր Սահակ հօր բոլոր ջանքը ապարդիւն գնաւեցաւ նախարարների անմտութիւնը զապելու եւ նրանց հասկացնելու, թէ ո՛րքան մեծ չարիք են գործում: Նրանք Սահակին եւս մատնեցին, եւ պարսից արքայի ձեռքով գրկեցին նրան կաթողիկոսական աթոռից: Եւ այսպէս, Հայաստանի հաստատութեան երկու հիմքերը—արքայական գահը եւ հայրապետական աթոռը—երկուսն էլ կործանվեցան: Թէ Սահակը եւ թէ Արտաշիրը աքսորված են Պարսկաստան: Մեր անտէր հայրենիքը այժմ մահուան տագնապի մէջ է գրանրվում. պէտք է օգնութիւն հասցնել:

— Ի՞նչով,—հարցրեց Պարոյրը սառն կերպով:

Երիտասարդը փոխանակ պատասխանելու, իր սուր աչքերով նայեց հռետորի երեսին, կարծես, ուզում էր ասել. մի՞թէ դուք չէ՞ք իմանում, թէ ի՛նչով:

— Ի՞նչով,—դարձեալ կրկնեց հռետորը:—Գնում էք կռուելո՞ւ պարսիկների հետ:

— Ինչո՛ւ չէ, եթէ հարկաւոր կը լինի,—պատասխանեց երիտասարդը յայտնի վրդովմունքով, որ պատճառեց նրա մէջ հռետորի սառնասրտութիւնը:

Հռետորը նկատելով այդ, ասաց.

—Գնացէք, գովում եմ ձեր եռանդը:

Երիտասարդը աւելի գայրացաւ:

—Պարո՛յր,—գոչեց նա,—ձեր մէջ սառել է հայկական արիւնը, դուք մեր հայրենիքի համար կորած մարդ էք: Ձեզ պատմում են այն թշուառութիւնները, որ պատահել են մեր աշխարհում եւ դուք սառնասրտութեամբ լսում էք: Դուք փոխվել էք, դուք շատ էք փոխվել: Դուք, որ մի քանի օր առաջ ձեր պերճախոսութեամբ հիացրիք ամբողջ Աթէնքը,—դուք այժմ շատ վատ էք խոսում այն լեզուով, որով խոսում էիք մի ժամանակ ձեր ծնողների հետ: Հելլենամոլութիւնը ձեր մէջ այն աստիճան զարգացել է, որ դուք փոխել էք մինչեւ անգամ ձեր անունը: Ձեզ ձեր հայրենիքում Պարոյր էին կոչում, իսկ այստեղ կոչվում էք Պրոյերեսիոս:

Հռետորը զգացվեցաւ: Երիտասարդը շարունակեց.

—Ես իրաւունք եմ համարում յանդիմանել ձեզ, Պարոյր, թէեւ տարիքով եւ դիրքով շատ մեծ էք ինձանից: Բայց մի՛ մոռացէք, որ դուք եւս այն երիտասարդներից մէկն էիք, որոնք գիտութեան առաքելութիւն անունով թողեցին հայրենիքը—որոնք ուխտեցին մեր Սահակ հոր եւ Մեսրոպի առջեւ գնալ, աշխարհէ աշխարհ պրտոտել, եւ գիտութեան պաշար հաւաքելով, յետոյ վերադառնալ հայրենիքը լուսաւորել։ Դուք, ես եւ մեր բոլոր ընկերները ամէն գոհողութիւններ յանձն առնելով, անցանք Եղեսիա, Անտիորքիա, Բիւզանդիա, Աղեքսանդրիա, Հռոմ եւ Աթէնք, այցելեցինք գիտութեան բոլոր տաճարները եւ յագեցրինք մեր ծարաւը։ Նպատակի մեծութիւնը բորբոքեց մեր եռանդը, գաղափարի վսեմութիւնը մեզ ուժ եւ զօրութիւն բաշխեց։ Մեզանից ամէն մէկը նշանաւոր գտնվեցաւ իր ասպարէզի մէջ։ Իմ քեռորդի ընկեր Դաւիթը² Բիւզանդիայում, Մարկիանոս կայսրի ներկայութեամբ, մրցութեան մէջ, իր անսահման գիտութեամբ լռեցրեց բոլոր փիլիսոփաներին եւ «անյաղթ փիլիսոփայ» անուն ստացաւ։ Եզնիկը,³ Յովսէփը,⁴ Ղեւոնդը,⁵ Կորիւնը⁶ զարմացրին Մաքսիմիանոս եպիսկոպոսին իրանց բարձր աստուածաբանական հմտութեամբ։ Իմ եղբայր

---

2 Դաւիթ անյաղթը յայտնի է իր փիլիսոփայական ինքնուրոյն եւ թարգմանական ամենահետաքրքիր աշխատութիւններով, որոնց մէջ նշանաւոր է «Սահմանաց գիրք կամ Սահմանք իմաստասիրութիւն»։

3 Եզնիկ Կողպացի, յայտնի է իր «Եղծ աղանդոց» գրքով, որով հերքում է իր ժամանակի կեղծ փիլիսոփայութիւնները, եւ գլխաւորապէս պարսից մոգական աղանդը։

4 Յովսէփ, յետոյ կաթողիկոս հայոց, գումարեց Արտաշատի ժողովը եւ Վարդանանց պատերազմա հրատարակեց ընդդէմ պարսից բռնութեան։

5 Ղեւոնդ երէց, իր հայրենասիրութեամբ յայտնի գտնվեցաւ Վարդանանց պատերազմի ժամանակ։

6 Կորիւն, Աստուածաշունչ գրող նշանաւոր թարգմանիչներրից մէկն էր, յետոյ վրաց եպիսկոպոս դարձաւ, երբ տակաւին վրացիք եկեղեցուց բաժանված չէին, գրեց իր վարժապետի՝ Մեսրոպի վարքի պատմութիւնը։

Մամբրէն,[7] Եղիշէն,[8] Ղազար Փարպեցին[9] նոյնպէս նշանաւոր հանդիսացան եւ որպէս հզոր աստուածաբաններ, եւ որպէս խորին գիտնականներ: Ես ուրիշ շատ երիտասարդների մասին չեմ խոսում, որոնք նոյնպէս դեպի արեւմուտք դիմեցին իրանց ուսումը կատարելագործելու նպատակով, եւ զարմանալի յառաջադիմութիւն գործեցին:—Այժմ յիշեալ երիտասարդները, լսելով մեր աշխարհի աղետները, մասամբ վերադառձել են հայրենիքը, մնացածներն եւս շտապում են գնալ: Նրանք տանում են իրանց հետ մի նոր գէնք Հայաստանը փրկելու, եւ դա է— լուսաւորութիւնը:

Հռետորը, որ բոլոր ժամանակը խորին ուշադրութեամբ լսում էր, կամաց հարցրեց.

—Դուք կարծում էք, որ լուսաւորութիւնը կը փրկէ՞ Հայաստանը:

—Ոչ միայն կարծում եմ, այլ համոզուած եմ, —ջերմութեամբ պատասխանեց երիտասարդը:

—Դուք, երեւի մոռացել էք, թէ վերջին ժամանակներում ինչ դժբախտ անցքեր անցան մեր աշխարհում: Հայաստանի բախտաւորութիւնը

---

7 Մամբրէ, որ կոչվում է «վարձանց» նշանաւոր է իր պատմական եւ քերականական աշխատութիւններով:

8 Եղիշէ, բացի սուրբ գրոց զանազան մեկնութիւններից, գըրեց Վարդանանց պատմութիւնը:

9 Ղազար Փարպեցի, յայտնի է իր հետաքրքիր հայոց պատմութիւնով եւ առ Վահան Մամիկոնեանը գրած թղթով, որի մէջ երեւում է ժամանակի խառարախիստ կղերի հալածանքը դեպի ճշմարիտ անձնանուէր գործիչ-ները:

միայն նրանում էր, որ այդ ժամանակ հայրապետական աթոռի վրա բազմած էր մի հանճարեղ մարդ, որպիսին էր մեր հայր Սահակ պարթեւը։ Նա արծուի սրատեսությամբ նախադիտում էր այն սարսափելի վտանգը, որ սպառնում էր մեր հայրենիքին։ Նա տեսնում էր Արշակունեացգահի մօտալուտ անկումը, տեսնում էր, որ Հայաստանը պիտի բաժանվի յոյների եւ պարսիկների մէջ, որոնք մինը միւսից աւելի վնասակար պէտք է լինէին։ Նա տեսնում էր եւ մի այլ դժբախտութիւն, որ Ս. Գրիգոր Լուսավորչի հայրապետական աթոռը պէտք է ժառանգեն կեղծաւորները, շահասէրները եւ դաւաճանները։ Հայրենիքի երկու հզոր պաշտպանների— հոգեւոր եւ մարմնաւոր իշխանութեան—վախճանը հասած էր տեսնում։ Այդ ժամանակ պէտք է օգնութեան հասնէր մի վիրկութիւն, որ լրացնէր այդ մեծ կորուստը, այսինքն հոգեւոր եւ մարմնաւոր իշխանութեան անկմանը։ Եւ այդ վիրկութիւնը սկսեց որոնել նա ժողովրդի կրրթութեան եւ լուսաւորութեան մէջ։ Եւ այդ էր գրլխաւոր շարժառիթը, որ նա ամենայն ջանքով սկսեց մեր աշխարհում ուսում տարածել,—ուսում մայրենի լեզուով։

Հռետորը լուռ էր, մատներով իր մօրուքի հետ խաղալով։ Երիտասարդը շարունակեց.

—Մեր Սահակ հօր նախորդները խիստ սահմանափակ եւ խախուտ հիմքերի վրա էին

դրել ժողովրդի կրթութեան գործը: Քրիստոնէ-
ութեան հետ նրանք մտցրին մեր մէջ յունաց
եւ ասորոց դպրութիւնը: Մեր առաջին վարժա-
պետները եղան յոյները եւ ասորիները: Գրում
էինք, կարդում էինք նրանց լեզուներով: Մեր ե-
կեղեցում անգամ տիրապետում էր օտար լեզու:
Սուրբ գրքերի ընթերցանութիւնը լսում էինք կամ
յունաց կամ ասրաց լեզուներով: Մի կողմից էլ
պարսիկն էր աշխատում իր լեզուն մեր մէջ մտցնել, որպէս դպրոցների եւ դիւանների պաշտօ-
նական լեզու: Մեր Սահակ հայրը պարզ տեսնում էր թէ ինչ մեծ չարիք կարող էր առաջանալ
այդ բոլորից: Մայրենի լեզուն հետզհետէ մեռնում էր,—մեռնում էր նրա հետ եւ ազգութիւնը:
Եւ դրա մէջն էր Հայաստանի իսկական մահը:
Հայը կորցնելով իր լեզուն, կը լուծվեր, կանհե-
տանար այն ազգերի մէջ, որոնց լեզուով խոսում
էր: Վտանգի մեծութիւնը սարսափելի էր: Եւ մեծ
Հայրապետը աշխատեց վտանգի առաջը առնել:
Նա գիտեր, որ հայր կորցնելով իր անկախու-
թիւնը, մի ժամանակ դարձեալ կարող էր ան-
կախութիւն ձեռք բերել, եթէ ազգը կենդանի կը
մնար: Բայց հայր կորցնելով իր լեզուն, կը դա-
դարէր ապրել իբրեւ առանձին ազգ,—նա կը
լինէր յոյն, ասորի, պարսիկ, կամ այն ազգերից
մէկը, որոնց լեզուով խոսում էր: Այդ մեծ չա-
րիքի առաջը առնելու համար ձեռք առին ժողովրդի կրթութեան գործը: Հարկաւոր էր ամեն

ինչ հայացնել, ամեն ինչ ազգային դարձնել: Մեր Սահակ հայրը իր ընդարձակ նպատակների մէջ աջակից ունեցաւ մի գործունեայ մարդ. որպիսին էր Մեսրոպը: Նա շտապեց ճնարել հայերի համար նոր տառեր, որպէս զի հայերը այլեւս յունաց, ասորոց եւ պարսից տառերով չգրէին: Սկսեցին նոյն տառերով թարգմանել սուրբ գրքերը, որպէս զի, եկեղեցու մէջ եւս տիրապետէր հայոց լեզուն եւ գիրը: Սկսեցին ամեն տեղ դպրոցներ բաց անել եւ հայոց գրով ու հայոց լեզուով կրթել մանուկներին:

—Յոյները եւ պարսիկները, որոնք արդէն Հայաստանը իրանց ճանկերի մէջ էին բռնել, եւ պատրաստվում էին ազգովին եւս կլանել նըրան,—այդ երկու ահեղ պետութիւնները չէին կարող չնկատել այն հզոր ընդդիմադրութիւնը, որ Հայաստանի հետաութես Հայրապետը պատրաստում էր նրանց նենգաւոր քաղաքականութեան առաջը առնել: Յոյները սկսեցին արգելել Հայաստանի այն մասում, որ իրանց գերիշխանութեան ներքոյ էր գտնվում, հայոց դպրոցներ բաց անել: Ձեզ պէտք է յայտնի լինի, թէ ո՛րքան հալածանքներ կրեց, ո՛րքան բանակցութիւններ ունեցաւ մեր Սահակ հայրը Բիւզանդիայի բարձր դռան հետ այդ մասին, մինչեւ Մեսրոպը նրա թոռ Վարդանի[10] հետ ստիպվեցան

---

10 Վարդան Մամիկոնեանը Սահակ Պարթեւի թոռն էր:

անձամբ Բիւզանդիա գնալ եւ կայսրից ու յունաց Ատտիկոս եպիսկոպոսից թոյլտութիւն խնդրել դպրոցներ բանալու համար, որը եւ ստացան մեծ դժուարութեամբ: Նոյն դժուարութիւններից աւելի սաստիկը բարձրացրեց պարսից կառավարութիւնը: Նա ուղարկեց ազգով հայ Մերուժան չարագործին եւ նրա ձեռքով այրել տուեց մեր գրքերը, եւ նրա ձեռքով աշխատում էր մացնել մեր նորահաստատ դպրոցներում մոգութեան ուսումը ու պարսից լեզուն:

Հռետորը շարունակում էր իր մատներով խաղալ մօրուքի հետ: Երիտասարդը առաջ տարաւ իր խօսքը.

—Մրցութիւնը յունաց եւ պարսից քաղաքականութեան հետ սաստիկ էր, իսկ ուժերը անհաւասար: Մեր Սահակ հօրը եւ Մեսրոպին հարկաւոր էին լաւ պատրաստուած ուժեր: Եւ այդ մտքով նրանք ընտրեցին քեզ, ինձ եւ իրանց յառաջադեմ աշակերտներից շատերին, եւ ուղարկեցին Բիւզանդիա, Աղեքսանդրիա, Հռոմ, Աթէնք բարձր ուսում ստանալու համար: Մենք անցանք քաղաքներ, որ յունական գիտութիւնը ստանալով, վերադառնանք մեր հայրենիքը, եւ իրանցից ստացած զէնքերով իրանց հետ պատերազմենք:

—Դա շատ նպատակայարմար միջոց է,— պատասխանեց հռետորը դադարելով խաղալ իր մօրուքի հետ:

—Բայց այդ զինուորներից մէկն էլ դուք պետք է լինիք,—պատասխանեց երիտասարդը ուղիղ հռետորի աչքերի մէջ նայելով:—Ես հենց դրա համար էլ եկայ ձեզ մօտ, որ միասին գնանք:

Հռետորը խորին վարանման մէջ ընկաւ: Նա այդ առաջարկութիւնը չէր սպասում երիտասարդից: Նա չգիտէր, ինչ պատասխանել:

Երիտասարդը խօսեց:

—Հասկանում եմ ձեր լռութեան եւ մտատանջութեան պատճառը, Պարոյր, բայց համաձայնվել ձեզ հետ չեմ կարող: Այն փառքը, այն հռչակը, որ դուք վայելում էք այստեղ շլացրել են ձեզ: Թողնել այդ բոլորը եւ գնալ թշուառ հայրենիքը, ուր շատ զոհողութիւններ է պահանջվում գործիչներից,—դա վախեցնում է ձեզ: Մեր ընկերները Դաւիթ անյաղթը, Եղիշէն, Եզնիկը, Ղազար Փարպեցին, Կորիւնը, իմ եղբայր Մամբրէն, Յովսէփիր, Ղեւնդը, մի խոսքով, բոլոր ուսանողները, որոնք զանազան երկրներում էին գտնվում, այժմ վերադարձել են կամ վերադառնալու վրա են: Մնացել ենք ես եւ դուք. Գրնանք, չյապաղենք, հայրենիքը կոչում է մեզ: Գրնանք գիտութիւն եւ լուսաւորութիւն տարածենք մեր աշխարհում, բաց անենք մեր հայրենակից- ների աչքերը, սովորեցնենք նրանց, որ հասկանան իրանց չարն ու բարին,—հասկանան, թէ ո'րպիսի անդունդի եզրում են կանգնած, որ գրլորվելով նրա մէջ, պիտի կործեն յաւիտեան:

Դուք այնպիսի զօրեղ հանճար ունէք, որ մնալով այստեղ, ես հաւատացած եմ, աւելի եւս կը բարձրանաք, եւ զուցէ առաջինը կը լինէք մեր ժամանակի փիլիսոփաների ու հոետորների մէջ։ Բայց դրանից ի՞նչ օգուտ ձեր հայրենիքին։

—Դրանից կ'օգտվի մարդկութիւնը,—պատասխանեց հռետորը երկար լռութիւնից յետոյ։ —Ես ծառայելով գիտութեանը, միեւնոյն ժամանակ ծառայում եմ ամբողջ աշխարհին։

—Այդ իրաւ է,—ասաց երիտասարդը փոքր ինչ տաքացած կերպով։—Բայց դուք չէ՞ք ընդունում որ մի առանձին պարտաւորութիւն ունէք դէպի ձեր հայրենիքը եւ դէպի ձեր հայրենակիցները։

—Ընդունում եմ, բայց իմ նպատակը շատ ընդարձակ է։ Գործեցէք դուք, կամ ով որ ցանկանում է ձեզ հետ, փոքրիկ շրջաններում, կամենում եմ ասել՝ մարդկութեան առանձին բաժինների մէջ, որ դուք ազգ էք կոչում։ Բայց իմ հայրենիքը ամբողջ աշխարհն է, իսկ իմ հայրենակիցները—ամբողջ մարդկութիւնը։

Կրակոտ երիտասարդը զայրացած կերպով կանգնեց.

—Դա մի կեղծաւոր պատճառաբանութիւն է, Պարոյր,—ասաց նա եւ սաստիկ վրդովմունքից նրա հզոր ձայնը կտրատվում էր։—Դուք, այսպէս խոսողներդ, գիտութեան փարիսեցիներ էք։ Մասնաւորի համար անրնդունակ լինելով գործել, միշտ ընդհանուրի անունով էք խոսում, ինչպես իրանց մասնաւոր պարտքը վատ վճարողները, ընդհանուր սեպհականութիւն են քարոզում: Ես յոյս ունէի, որ դուք երկար խոսել չէիք տալ ինձ, այլ լսելով թշուառ հայրենիքի դրութիւնը, կ՚ընկերանայիք ինձ հետ եւ հենց այս առաւօտ կը թողնէիք Աթէնքը: Բայց ես աւելի խոսեցի, քան հարկաւոր էր, եւ դա իզուր ժամանակի կորուստ եղաւ ինձ համար: Գիտութեան սէրը եւ հանրա-մարդկային լուսաւորութիւն տարածելու զազափարը չէ, որ կապում է ձեզ Աթէնքի հետ,—այլ սնոտի փառքը եւ այն մագաղաթի կտորը, որ դրած է ձեր սեղանի վրա...

Այդ խոսքերի հետ նա ձեռքը մեկնեց եւ վեր առեց կայսրի հրովարտակը, որ նոյն օրը ստացել էր հռետորը, եւ բարձրացնելով ասաց.

—Ահա, այդ մագաղաթի կտորն է, որ հր-րապուրում է ձեզ: Արեւելքի եւ արեւմուտքի կայսրը այդ հրովարտակով հրաւիրում է ձեզ իր մօտ: Իսկ միւս կողմից, անբախտ հայրենիքը իմ բերանով կոչում է ձեզ: Դուք մերժում էք նրա ձայնը, եւ այդ պատճառով անարժան էք Հայաստանի զաւակ կոչվելու:

Վերջին խոսքերի հետ երիտասարդը հե-ռացաւ: Հռետորը շանթահարի նման մնաց ապ-շութեան մէջ:

Երիտասարդը Մովսես Խորենացին էր:

ԳԼՈՒԽ Գ

«Եւ մինչ նորա [Սահակ եւ Մեսրոպ զմերն
յուսային զգարձ եւ պատուասիրել իմով
ամենիմաստ արուեստիւ եւ կատարելա-
գոյն յարմարութեամբս, համայն եւ մեք
փութապէս դիմեալք ի Բիւզանդիոյ, յու-
սայաք հարասանեաց պարել, անվեհեր ե-
 րագութեամբ կրթեալք եւ առագաստի ա-
սել երգս, արդ փոխանակ խրախճանու-
թեանն ի վերայ գերեզմանի ողբս ասելով ողորմելի հառաչեմ, ուր եւ ոչ տեսու-
թեանն ժամանեցի աչաց նոցա կափուց-
ման եւ լսել զվերջին բարբառն եւ զօրհնու-
թիւն:»

—Խորենացի

Գիշերային խաւարը պատել էր Արարատեան
դաշտը: Օշական գիւղի սուրբ Մեսրոպի անա-
պատում ոչ մի լոյս չէր երեւում: Ամեն արարած
խոր քնի մեջ էր, ամեն ինչ ընկղմուած էր խուլ
լռութեան մեջ: Չէր լսվում եւ գիշերահսկիկ
անապատականների մշտական սաղմոսերգու-
թիւնը, միայն մի մատուռի մեջ ծխվում էր լու-
սային կանթեղը, եւ որպէս տխուր հոգու թախծալի արտայայտութին, տարածում էր իր շուրջը
աղօտ լուսաւորութին:

103

Մատուռի մէջ դրած էր մի շիրիմ: Կանթեղի լոյսը ուղիղ թափվում էր նրա վրա եւ երեւան էր հանում նրա անշուք կազմութիւնը: Շիրիմը կառուցուած էր սեւ քարից եւ, կարծես թէ, փոխաբերական իմաստով արտայայտում էր այն մեծ մարդու հոգեկան դառնութիւնը, որ անմխիթար տրտմութեամբ իջել էր այդ ագաւոր դամբարանի մէջ:

Շիրիմի մօտ, մերկ հատակի վրա ծունր իջած, խոնարհուած էր մի մարդ: Նրա գլուխը հանգչում էր սառն տապանաքարի վրա, եւ երկայն, թաւամազ ծամերը ծածկել էին նրա սեւ մակերեւոյթը: Այդ դրութեան մէջ նա անշարժ էր, անշարժ էին եւ նրա թեւքերը, որոնցմով գրկել էր շիրիմը: Ոչ մի մրմունջ, ոչ մի հառաչանք չէր աղմկում այդ ողբանուէր ագաւորի տրխուր լռութիւնը, միայն կիսախուփ աչքերից արտասուքի մեղմ վտակները հոսում էին սառը քարի վրա:

Երկար նա, այնպէս գետնատարած, գրկել էր շիրիմը, երկար նա, այնպէս ճակատը դրած սառը քարի վրա, կպել էր նրան եւ, կարծես, աշխատում էր դուրս կոչել մթին դամբարանի միջից այդ մեծ հանգուցեալի ուրուականը,—աշխատում էր տեսնել նրան, խոսել նրա հետ եւ թափել նրա առջեւ իր սրտի վշտերը:

Այնպես գետնատարած, լուռ ողբում էր նա, մինչեւ անապատի զանգակատնից լսելի եղաւ վաղորդեան կոչնակի թախծալի հնչիւնը: Այդ մեղմ հնչիւնը սթափեցրեց նրան իր հոգեկան խորին յափշտակութիւնից: Գլուխը վեր բարձրացրեց եւ մի առանձին սոսկումով նայեց իր շուրջը: Օրը լուսանում էր... Կարծես նա վախենում էր, որ իրան կը տեսնէին այստեղ: Ուտի կանգնեց...

Ո՞վ էր այդ գիշերային այցելուն, այդ ն՞ւմ դամբարանի վրա էր թափում իր դառն արտասուքը:

— Խաղաղութի՞ն քո սուրբ ոսկերացը, ո՛վ երանելի հայր,— բացականչեց նա, սգաւոր հայացքը ձգելով շիրիմի վրա:— Երկար ճանապար- հորդութիւններից յետոյ, քո դժբախտ աշակերտը վերադառնալով հայրենիք, մեծ յոյս ունէր՝ քո գրկի մէջ մխիթարութիւն գտնել եւ մխիթարել քեզ: Բայց նա շառժանագաւ քո քաղցր տեսու- թեանը, չը լսեց քո բարի շրթունքների վերջին օրհնութիւնը, եւ ոչ իրձեռքով փակեց այն սրա- տես աչքերը, որոնք հայրենիքի հեռու եւ մերձ աղէտները տեսնելով, փոխանակ արտասուք թափելու, ամեն ջանքով աշխատում էին դարման տանել: Քո պատուիրանաց համեմատ, գնացի, անցայ երկրից երկիր, քաղաքից քաղաք, այցե- լեցի գիտութեան բոլոր տաճարները, եւ լի հրձ- տութիւններով վերադարձայ իմ հայրենիքը: Բայց ո՞վ այսուհետեւ զին կը դնէ այն մտաւոր մթերքին, որ բերել եմ օտար աշխարհներից:[11] Դու եւ քո վեհափառ գործակիցը (Սահակ) միայն հասկանում էիք, թէ ի՞նչ է ճշմարիտ լոյսը եւ ուղիղ վարդապետութիւնը: Անգութ մահը միաժամանակ խաւարացրեց այդ երկու արեգակները, եւ մութը տիրեց հայոց երկրին: Լաւերը գնացին, այժմ նրանց փոխարինում են վատերը: Մեր սուրբ Լուսավորիչ հօր ապօրը ժառանգել են աստրինները, կամ այնպիսի հայ հայրապետ- ներ, որոնք աշխատում են աւելի բռնակալ պարսից Դռանը հաճոյանալ, քան թէ Յիսուս Քրիստոսի սուրբ եկեղեցուն:[12] Մեր այժմեան վարդապետները,[13] որոնք պէտք է հոգեւոր եւ բարոյական ուղղութիւն տային ժողովրդին, ո- րոնք պէտք է ուսուցանէին նրան ճշմարիտը եւ արդարը,—իրանք աւելի եւս մոլորեցնում են ժո- ղովուրդը: Տգէտ են դրանք, եւ միեւնոյն ժամա- նակ ինքնահաւան: Առանց որեւիցէ մտաւոր եւ բարոյական արժանաւորութեան՝ ստացել են

---

11 «Ո՞վ այսուհետեւ զմերս յարգեացէ զուսումն, ո՞վ ուրա- խացի ընդ առաջադիմութիւն աշակերտիս, ո՞վ զհայրականն բարբառեցի զուարճութիւն...» —Խորենացի

12 «Ողորմի՞մ քեզ, եկեղեցի Հայաստանեայց, խռնացեալ ի բարեզարդութենէ բերմին, ի քաջէն գրկեալ ի հովուէ եւ ի հովուակցէ: Ոչ եւս Տեսանեմ զբանաւոր քո հօտ ի վայրի դալարոնջ եւ ոչ ի ջուրս հանգստեան սնեալ, եւ ոչ ի փարախս հաւաքեալ՝ զգուշանալով ի գայլոց, այլ ցրուեալ անապատաց եւ զահավիժութեանց»: —Խորենացի

13 «Վարդապետք տխմարք եւ ընդինքնահաւանք, անձամբ առ- եալ պատիւ եւ ոչ յԱստուծոյ կոչեցեալ, արծաթով ընտրեալք եւ ոչ Հոգւով, ոսկեսէրք, նախանձոտք, թողեալ զհեզութիւն, յորում Աստուած բնակէ, եւ գայլք եղեալ՝ զհիրեանց հօտս գիշատելով»: —Խորենացի

կարգ եւ աստիճան: Աւելի արծաթով են ընտր-
ված, քան թէ հոգույն սրբոյ շնորհիւ: Եւ այդ
պատճառով, իրանք եւս արծաթասէր են եւ նախանձոտ: Քրիստոնէական առաքինութիւնը բա-
ցակայ է նրանցից, եւ թողնելով հեզութիւնը,
որի մէջ Աստուած է բնակվում, իրանք գայլեր
են դարձել եւ իրանց հօտն են գիշատում: Մեր
կրօնաւորները,[14] մեր վանական աբեղաները, ո-
րոնք պէտք է ջերմ հաւատքի եւ եղբայրասի-
րութեան օրինակ տային ժողովրդին, որոնք
պէտք է վառէին նրա մէջ սիրոյ ու միաբանու-
թեան ոգին,—իրանք աւելի եւս երկպառակու-
թեան սերմեր են ցանում: Դրանք՝ միայն փարի-
սեցու կեղծաւորութեամբ, միայն արտաքին բա-
րեպաշտութեան դիմակով խաբում են ժողովրդին, բայց ներքուստ են՝ անապատ, պատուա-
սէր, քան թէ աստուածասէր: Իրանց՝ աշխարհի
վայելչութիւնից անջատուած եւ մարդկային հասարակութիւնից հեռացած ձեւացնելով, վանքերի խուլ պատերի մէջ վայելում են ամբողջ աշխարհը: Մեր վիճակաւորները,[15] որոնք պէտք է
պահպանէին ժողովրդի մէջ իրաւունքը եւ արդա-
րութիւնը, որոնք պէտք է հոգ տանէին եկեղեցու
բարեկարգութեան համար,—իրանք աւելի եւս

---

14 «Կրօնաւորք կեղծաւորք, անձնացոյցք, անապատք, պատ-
ուասէրք քան թէ աստուածասէրք»: —Խորենացի
15 «Վիճակաւորք հպարտք, դատասացք, զրաբանք, ծոյլք, ա-
տեղողք արունորից եւ վարդապետական բանից, սիրողք վա-
ճառաց եւ կատակերգութեանց»: —Խորենացի

խախտում են նրա հիմքերը: Եկեղեցու այդ ծույլ, անհոգ կառավարիչները իրանց ժամանակը վատնում են գրախոսութեամբ եւ կատակերգու- թիւններ լսելով խնջոյքների մէջ: Ատելի է նր- անց գիտութիւնը եւ վարդապետական խոսքը, եւ սիրելի է նրանց եկեղեցու խորհրդավածա- ռութիւնը: Սիմոնականութիւնը այդ շահասեր- ների ձեռքով իր ծայրահեղ անամօթութեանն է հասել: Չնչին մամօնայի համար նրանք ամեն տարի հարիւրներով եւ հազարներով բազմաց- նում են եկեղեցու անպիտան պաշտօնեաների թիւը: Յիշեալ անկարգ դաստիարակողների շր- նորհիւ, ի՞նչ տեսակ սերունդ է պատրաստվում այժմ, ի՞նչ է մեր դպրոցների աշակերտաց վի- ճակը:[16] Այլ եւս առաջուայ սէրը դէպի ճշմա- րիտ գիտութիւնը, եւ առաջուայ եռանդը դէպի օգտաւէտ ուսումը չէ մնացել: Մեր դպրոցները կրթում են մի ծույլ, դատարկամիտ սերունդ, որը դեռ ոչինչ չը սովորած, աշխատում է երեւելի աստուածաբան ձեւանալ, որը դեռ բոլորովին տգէտ լինելով սուրբ գրքերի մեկնութեան մէջ, սկսում է վարդապետութիւններ անել: Դպրոցը, այդ սուրբ եկեղեցու սուրբ նախագաւիթը, չէ սերմանում մանուկների սրտում այն մաքուր եւ սրբազան սերմերը, որ նրանք ապագայում

___
16 «Աշակերտնք հետզ առ ուսումն և փոյթք առ ի վարդապետել, որք նախ քան զտեսութիւնն աստուա-ծաբանք» —Խորենացի

եկեղեցու եւ հայրենիքի հաւատարիմ զաւակներ դառնային, որ նրանք ճանաչին իրանց պարտքը դէպի երկինքը եւ դէպի աշխարհըմարդկու- թիւնը: Այժմեան դպրոցը, ընդհակառակն, խեղ- դում, ոչնչացնում է մանուկների սրտում այն դե- րաբոյս ծիլերը, որոնք ապագայում աճելով եւ ծաղկելով, կարող էին բարի պտուղներ տալ...

Նա փոքր ինչ կանգ առեց եւ րոպէական լը- ռութիւնից յետոյ շարունակեց.

—Ահա այսպիսի անձանց ձեռքումն է եկե- ղեցու տնտեսութիւնը, եւ ժողովրդի հոգեւոր ու մտաւոր կրթութեան գործը: Իսկ մե՞նք:—Մենք այժմ համարվում ենք աղանդաւորներ:[17] Տգէտ, խաւարամիտ եւ կեղծաւոր կղերը հալածում է մեզ: Մեր գրաւոր աշխատութիւնները համարում են վնասակար.[18] մեր ուսումը, մեր վարդապետու- թիւնը համարում են մոլորեցուցիչ: Մի տէր, մի մեծ չը կայ, որ սանձահարէ այդ նախանձոտ, չարամիտ պարեգօտաւորների գրպարտութիւն- ները,[19] որոնք ամեն ստախօսութեամբ գրգռում

17 «Այլ ասեն, աղանդաւոր է: Եւ զայս ստէպ ձանուցանել ամե- նեցունց ճեպէին, զորս հաւատացուցեալ ի տկարամտաց՝ թերի վարդապետութիւն շնորհին որ էր ի յիս, հայեցուցանէին :»
—Ղազար Փարպեցի

18 Երանելի փիլիսոփոսն Մովսէս (Խորենացի), որ արդարեւ մինչդեռ էր ի մարմնի՝ ցանկ երկնային զօրացն էր քաղաքա- կից. ո՞չ ապաքէն ի տեղւոջէ ի տեղի աքեղեանդ Հայոց հալա- ծական արարին: Ո՞չ զլուսաւորիչն եւ զոգիտահալած զգր- եանս նորա առ անգիտութեան «փաթաղիկէս» կոչէին»...
—Ղազար Փարպեցի

19 «Ո՞վ կարկեացէ զլանդգնութիւնն ընդդէմ առողջ վարդա- պետութեանն հակառակ յարուցելոցն, որք ամենայն բանիւ

են միամիտ ժողովրդին մեր դէմ եւ արգելք են
դնում մեր գործունէութեանը: Դու, ո՛վ երանելի
հայր, քո հզօր գործակցի (սուրբ Սահակի) հետ,
ձեր աշակերտներից ստեղծեցիք եկեղեցական-
ների մի նոր սերունդ: Դրանց թիւը փոքր չէր:
Զբաղականանալով այն ուսումով, որ ստացել
էին նրանք ձեր հոգաբարձութեան ներքոյ, դու
եւ քո մեծ գործակիցը ուղարկեցիք նրանց օ-
տար երկրներում կատարելագործուելու: Նրանք
գնացին եւ վերադարձան գիտութեան մեծ պա-
շարով: Բայց ի՞նչ եղաւ նրանց վախճանը: Խա-
լարամիտ կղերը շատերին թոյլ չտուեց, որ ներս
մտնէին հայրենի երկրի սահմաններից,[20] եւ ո-
րոնք մտան՝ հալածուեցան... Այժմ հայրենիքի
այդ անձնազոհ մշակները թաքուստի մէջ են
ապրում եւ միայն գաղտնի են գործում: Նրանք
համարձակուին չունեն օտար աշխարհներից
բերած գիտութեան պաշարը ժողովրդին մատա-
կարարելու: «Թարգման» անունը մեր վերաբե-
րութեամբ ծաղրական եւ նախատական անուն

քակտեալք եւ քայքայեալք՝ յոլովս փոփոխեն վարդապետս
եւ բազում գիրս... Ո՞վ զնոսա ընբերանեացէ սաստելով, եւ
զմեզ սփոփեացէ գովելով, եւ չափ դնէ բանի եւ լռութեան»:
—Խորենացի

20 «Անարատ եւ յամենեցունց յարգելի յոյսն՝ տէր Խոսրովիկ,
չեւ եւս հասեալ ի սահմանս մեր՝մինչդեռ զայր ի ճանապարհի եւ լուան (աբեցայբ) որպէս ի վերայ թշնամւոյ ընդդէմ
զինեցան՝ ասելով. «Ահա ո՞ւր գայ միւս թարգմանն»: Եւ օրհ-
նելոյն ի հեռաստանէ լուեալ զդռնչիւն մահաձայն աղեղանցն՝
առօթեաց առ Բարձրեալն եւ վաղվաղակի ընկալաւ զինն-
դիրն, որում եւ տենչալի ն՞շխարացն այլբ՝ եւ ոչ մեք, արժանի
եղեն ընդունակութեան:» —Ղազար Փարպեցի

է դարձել ճնամոլ կղերի բերանում: Մենք, որ
ամեն ջանք գործ էինք դնում, աշխատում էինք,
եւ այժմ աշխատում ենք, որ հայր հայոց լեզուով
խոսէ իր տան մէջ, որ հայր հայոց լեզուով ա-
ղօթէ Աստուծոյ տան մէջ,—մենք, որ աշխատում
էինք, եւ այժմ աշխատում ենք՝ ամեն ինչ հայացնել, ամեն բանի ազգային գոյն տալ,—մենք, որ
քո ստեղծած տառերով թարգմանեցինք բոլոր
սուրբ գրքերը եւ այդ աստուածապարգեւ տա-
ռերը աշխատում էինք մտցնել հայոց կեանքի
եւ գործածութեան մէջ,—մենք, որ մեր ամեն ուժերը գործ էինք դնում, որպէս զի մեր դպրոցները, մեր եկեղեցին ազատ պահենք նենգաւոր
յոյնի, ժանտ պարսկի եւ խաբեբայ ասորու վր-
նասական ազդեցութիւններից,—մենք այժմ հալածվում ենք մեր աշխատութիւնների համար, եւ
հալածվում ենք ովքերից,—մերայիններից...

Վերջին խոսքերը արտասանելու ժամանակ, նրա ձայնը վրդովմունքից խեղդուեցաւ եւ
նրա աչքերում փայլեց բարկութեան կրակը:

—Նայիր, ո՛վ սուրբ հայր, նայիր հոգւոյ աչքերով, տե՛ս իմ ցաւալի վիճակը: Այդ ճանապարհորդական ցուպը ձեռքիս, այդ պարկը ուսիս, այդ
ճնոտի հագուստը հագիս, մի ողորմելի մուրաց-
կանի նման, եկել, հասել եմ այստեղ: Մեր վանքերը, որոնց մէջ ամեն օտարական օթեւան եւ
անունդ է գտնում,—մեր վանքերը ինձ գիշերելու
անգամ մի անկիւն չէին տալիս, եւ շատերի մէջ

ինքս չէի համարձակվում մտնել, որպէս զի չընկնեմ չարամիտների որոգայթի մէջ... Շա՜տ օրեր քաղցած եմ մնացել, շա՜տ անգամ ստիպուած եմ եղել մօտենալ բարի զիւղացիների դռանը եւ մի պատառ հաց խնդրել։ Թաքցրել եմ իմ ո՛վ կամ ի՛նչ մարդ լինելս... Եւ այն մարդը, որ Բիւզանդիայում Մարկիանոս կայսրին զարմացնում էր իր իմաստութեամբ, եւ նրա հիւրասիրութիւնն էր վայելում,—այժմ այդ թշուառը իր հայրենիքում գլուխը ցոյց տալու համարձակութիւն չունի...

Նրա զայրացած դէմքի վրա դարձեալ նրշմարուեցան բարկութեան ցնցումներ, որոնց ռոպէական լռութիւնից յետոյ փոխարինեց խադաղ հեզութիւն։

—Իսկ այդ բոլոր հալածանքները չեն կարող վհատեցնել ինձ, չեն յուսահատուի եւ իմ ընկերները։ Մենք, որպէս անձնազոհ զինուորներ, ուխտել ենք պատերազմել խաւարի եւ տրգիտութեան դէմ,—ուխտել ենք պատերազմել վաճառուած կղերի դաւաճանութեան եւ չարիքների դէմ, այն կղերի, որ մեր արքունի զահը կործանող եւ մեր հայրապետական աթոռը խորտակող պարսկի ձեռքում այժմ մի յարմար գործիք է դարձել՝ մեր աշխարհի մնացած զօրութիւնները ոչնչացնելու համար...

Նա կրկին ծունր իջաւ շիրիմի մօտ եւ նրա շրթունքները համբոյր մատուցին սառը տապանաքարին:

—Երդվում եմ այս սուրբ շիրիմով,—բացականչեց նա,—եւ կրկնում եմ իմ ուխտը, որը կը մնայ անխախտ մինչեւ իմ կեանքի վերջին շունչը: Հալածանքը, նեղութիւնը չեն կարող մեղցնել այն հոգին, որը դու, ո՛վ երանելի հայր, ներշնչեցիր իմ սրտի մէջ: Ես միշտ հաւատարիմ կմնամ այն մեծ գործին, որի առաքելութեան համար կոչվեցայ: Քո բարձր նպատակը մեր հայրենիքի փրկութեան մասին, կրթութեան եւ լուսաւորութեան միջոցով, պէտք է իրագործուի: Այն հիմքը, որ հմուտ ձեռքով դրեցիր դու, —ես եւ իմ ընկերները կը շարունակենք նրա վրա շինուածքը: Մեր անբախտ աշխարհը կորցրեց քեզ, բայց քո հոգին եւ քո վսեմ մտքը կենդանի մնաց մեր սրտում: Դու եւ քո հզոր գործակիցը, իրաւ է, թողեցիք աշակերտների մի փոքրիկ եւ անպաշտպան խումբ, բայց այդ անշան խումբը իր փոքրամասնութեան մէջ մեծ եւ զօրաւոր կը լինի, որովհետեւ ներշնչուած է բարձր, հանրագգային գաղափարներով...

Անապատի զանգակներն սկսեցին աւելի եւ աւելի բարձր հնչել: Արշալոյսը շառագունել էր: Դրսից լսելի էր լինում նոր զարթնած թռչունների ձայնը:

Օտարականը կրկին եւ կրկին համբուրեց գերեզմանը, եւ վերջին անգամ իր տխուր հայացքը ձգելով սեւ տապանաքարի վրա, վերցրեց իր ճանապարհորդական ցուպն ու պարկը եւ զգուշութեամբ դուրս եկաւ մատուռից։

Անապատի մէջ կատարվում էր վաղորդեան ժամերգութիւնը։ Աբեղաներն աղօթում էին։ Ծերունի ժամկոչը՝ միայնակ նստած եկեղեցու դռան հանդէպ եւ բաւական զոռ իր վիճակից՝ նայում էր դէպի զանգակատան բարձրութիւնը, որի վրա աղաւնիներն այդ ժամանակ մի առանձին բաւականութեամբ սեթեւեթում էին միմեանց հետ։ Սպասաւորներից մէկը աւելում էր բակը։

Ժամկոչը հեռուից տեսաւ օտարականին։ Ուղեւորի ցուպը, մէջքին կապած պարկը եւ մաշուած հագուստը առիթ տուին նրան մտածել, թէ մի օրեիցէ մուրացկան պէտք է լինի, որ գիշերը պատսպարուել էր անապատում։ Բայց նրա մէջ կասկած պատճառեց մի բան, թէ ի՞նչու այդ մուրացկանն այդպէս վաղ առաւօտեան թողնում է անապատը, այն եւս առանց եկեղեցին մտնելու, կամ գոնէ նրա դուռը համբուրելու։ Նա կանչեց իր մօտ բակը աւելող սպասաւորին եւ հարցրեց։

—Տեսա՞ր այն մուրացկանին։

—Տեսայ,—պատասխանեց սպասաւորը կոդքը թորելով։—Նա դուրս եկաւ սուրբ Մեսրոպի մատուռից։

—Սուրբ Մեսրոպի մատուտի՞ց,—կրկնեց ժամկոչը զարմանալով։—Այնտեղ ի՞նչ էր շինում։

—Ի՞նչ պիտի շիներ,—ասաց սպասաւորը, շարունակելով կողքը քորել,—երեխի մտել էր իր հին վարժապետի գերեզմանի վրա «հոգւոց» կարդալու։

—Ո՞վ էր նա։

—Ո՞ր ճանաչեցի՞ք։

—Հարիւրաւոր մուրացկաններ են գալիս այստեղ, ո՞ր մէկին կարող ես ճանաչել։

—Նա մուրացկան չէր։

—Ապա ո՞վ էր։

—Մովսէսը։

—Ի՞նչ Մովսէս։

—Խորենացին։

Ժամկոչը մնաց շուարած։

—Աչքովդ տեսա՞ր, ճանաչեցի՞ր, խօսե-ցի՞ր նրա հետ։

—Քթովս խօ չէի տեսնի, հէր-օրհնած,—պատասխանեց սպասաւորը, այժմ միւս կողքը քորելով։—Հենց այս երկու աչքերովս տեսայ, լաւ ճանաչեցի, բայց չխօսեց ինձ հետ։ Ես նրան ճա-նաչում էի այն ժամանակից, երբ այսքան տղայ էր։

Վերջին խօսքերի միջոցին նա ձեռքը մի կանգուն բարձրաթեամբ բռնեց գետնի վրա, որ ցոյց տայ, թէ ինչ հասակի տղայ էր։

Ժամկոչը ձեռքով բազմախորհուրդ կերպով շփեց իր ճակատը եւ հազիւ լսելի ձայնով
ասաց.

—Մեր հայր-սուրբերը նրան որոնում էին...

—Նրան հիմա ինքը սատանան չի գտնի:

—Ինչո՞ւ:

—Դու չե՞ս իմանում, որ Հոռոմաստանից
նոր եկած վարդապետները բոլորն էլ կախարդ-
ներ են...

ԳԼՈՒԽ Դ

«Մի՛ ելս յայսմհետէ բարձր ի գլուխս պարծի Կեկրոպիա.

Ոչ է օրէն ընդ արեգական զաղոտալոյս կշռել ջահ.

Ոչ մահացուի ընդ Պրոյերեսեայ գալ ի պայքար հռետորական.

Որ զիւսօրէն նուաճեաց գերկիր ի ճարտասան բանիցն հանդէս:

Ի շանթեացն՝ յեղակարծուց սասանեցաւ Ատտիկատան.

Եւ ընդհանուր կոկովարան իմաստակաց կոկոզ կամարք՝

Տեղի ետուն Պրոյերեսիայ. տալ ետ տեղի եւ ինքն բախտ.

Անշքեցան փառքն Աթենայ պայծառք՝ ի դառն ի յօրիասէն.

Փախերուք այսուհետեւ ի Կեկրոպիայ, մանկունք համբակք:»

—Գրիգոր Ասատուրեան

Մի բարձրահասակ մարդ, պատկառելի դեմքով, համարձակ ելեւմուտ էր անում Կոնստանդ կայսրի շքեղ արքունիքը: Պալատականները ամենայն ակնածութեամբ ոտքի էին կանգնում նրա առջեւ եւ խորին յարգանքով դողչունում էին նրան:

Նա ոչ մեծահոչակ զօրավար էր եւ ոչ երկըրների կուսակալ։ Նա ոչ կայսրի գերիշխանութեան ներքոյ գտանվող մի թագաւոր էր եւ ոչ իշխան։ Նրա պարզ, անշուք հագուստն անգամ չէր ցոյց տալիս, որ նա աշխարհի աստիճաններով օժտուած մէկը լինէր։ Երբեմն տեսնում էին նրան բոբիկ ոտներով պալատը մտնելիս. երբեմն նա գլխարկ չունէր, եւ երկայն ծամերը կապված էին լինում հասարակ վարսակալով։ Բայց դարձեալ ամէն գլուխ խոնարհվում էր նրա առջեւ։

Այսպէս անփոյթ կերպով, այսպէս աշխարհի կարգերը արհամարհելով, մուտք ունեն հզօրների պալատը երկու տեսակ անձնաւորութիւններ միայն՝—մարգարէն եւ փիլիսոփան։ Այդ մարդը փիլիսոփայ էր եւ հռետոր։

Կայսերական սեղանի ամենապատուաւոր տեղում նա բազմող ունէր։ Այն սեղանը, որի շուրջը երկրների թագաւորները ոտքի վրա սպասաւորութիւն էին անում,—այն սեղանը իրան մեծ պատիւ էր համարում այդ մարդու ներկայութիւնը։ Բայց այն ճոխ սեղանը, որ լի էր աշխարհի ամենահագուագիւտ բարիքներով, որի վրա ոսկեայ եւ արծաթեայ ամանների մէջ դըրած էին երկրների ամենաթանկագին ընպելիները,—այդ սեղանը չէր գրաւում նրա ախորժակը։ Նրա խմածը պարզ ջուր էր, իսկ կերածը ցամաք հաց թարմ պտուղներով։

Այդ մարդը Հռովմի մեջ հիւր էր: Նա կայսրի պալատը կենդանացնում էր իր իմաստուն պերճախոսութեամբ, իսկ քաղաքների թագուհուն մտք եւ հոգի էր տալիս իր հռետորական ճառերով: Ամեն օք խորին հրճուանքով սպասում էր, որ Կիկերոնը կրկին յարութիւն է առել. ամեն օք, սկսեալ ծերակոյտի ատենականից մինչեւ վերջին քաղաքացին, շտապում էր նրա դասախոսութիւնները լսելու:

Ամբողջ վեց ամիս նա մտաւոր եւ հոգեկան անուրդ էր բաշխում Հռովմին, եւ երբ պետք է մեկնէր այնտեղից, քաղաքը վճռեց յաւերժացնել նրա յիշատակը պատուի արձանով:

Քաղաքի աւելի ակնյայտնի հրապարակներից մէկի վրա կանգնեցրած էր պղնձեայ արձանը, որը հռետորի հասակի չափը եւ նմանութիւնն ունէր: Բացման հանդէսը կատարվեցաւ ամենափառաւոր կերպով, որպիսին ընդունակ է կատարել Հռովմի տօնասէր ճաշակը. Երբ բարձրացրին արձանը ծածկող քօղը, նրա պատուանդանի վրա կարդացվեցաւ հետեւեալ մակագրութիւնը:

Միեւնույն օրերում, երբ կայսրի պալատի բոլոր դռները բաց էին հռետորի առջեւ, երբ նա համարձակ ելումուտ էր անում այնտեղ որպես մի հարգելի հիւր,—նոյն պալատի դռան առջեւի հրապարակի վրա, համարեա ամեն օր, դեգերում էին երկու արեւելցիք: Նրանց հագուստից, գէնքերից եւ այլ նշաններից երեւում էր, որ այդ օտարականները հասարակ մարդիկ չէին, այլ, կամ փոքրիկ թագաւորներ էին, կամ երկրների տիրապետող իշխաններ: Նրանցից իրաքանչիրը ունէր իր հետ մի խումբ թիկնապահներ եւ սպասաւորներ, իրաքանչիրը կրում էր կարմիր կօշիկներ եւ կարմիր գոյնով վարտիք, որ նշան էին նախարարի: Մի շաբաթից աւելի կը լինէր, որ այդ օտարականները երեւում էին պալատի դռան առջեւ, բայց դեռ մուտք չէին գործել արքունիքը եւ չէին ներկայացել կայսրին, թէեւ յատկապէս այդ նպատակով եկած էին: Նրանք մի քանի անգամ միայն տեսնվել էին փոքր Ասիայի կուսակալի հետ, որը միշտ յուսադրում էր, թէ օր կը որոշէ նրանց ներկայացնելու կայսրին: Բայց օրերը անցնում էին եւ նրանց խնդիրքը մնում էր անկատար: Երբ օտարականները շատ թախանձում էին, մի անգամ կուսակալը հեգնութեամբ ասաց նրանց՝ «Կայսրի դռանը թագաւորներին անգամ ամիսներով եւ տարիներով սպասել են տալիս, բայց դուք՝ հայերդ, երեւի շատ անհամբեր էք»...

Համարեա միեւնոյն օրերում, երբ հիւսողը ստացաւ այն մեծ պատիւը, երբ վերջացած էր արձանի բացման հանդէսը եւ երբ նա պատրաստվում էր թողնել Հռովմը,—այդ ժամանակ երկու օտարական իշխանները ներկայացան նրան: Առանց յայտնելու, թէ իրանք ովքեր են եւ ինչ նպատակով են եկել, տուեցին նրան մի նամակ, որ գրել էր հայոց կաթողիկոս սուրբ Վրթանէսը: Հայրապետական պատշաճաւոր օրհնութիւններից եւ բարեմաղթութիւններից յետոյ նամակը սկսւում էր հետեւեալ խոսքերով.

«Մե՞ծ փառք եւ պարծանք է հայոց ազգի եւ Հայաստանի համար, որ իր հարազատ զաւակներից մէկը իր իմաստութեամբ զարմացնում է ամբողջ արեւելքն ու արեւմուտքը, իսկ իր հանճարով բարձր պատիւ է վայելում Հռովմի օգնտափառ կայսրի պալատում: Այսպիսի պատուի չէ արժանացել եւ ոչ մի աշխարհական, որ Հռովմէական Կայսրութեան սահմանները տարածեցին դէպի Ասիայ եւ Ափրիկայ խորքերը:

«Ձեզ անշուշտ յայտնի պետք է լինի մեր Տրդատ հզոր արքայի բարեկամական հարաբերութիւնները Հռովմի այժմեան կայսրի հօր՝ Կոստանդիանոս մեծի հետ: Ձեզ յայտնի պետք է լինի եւ «Դաշանց թուղթը», որ գրւեցաւ եւ կնքւեցաւ այդ երկու ինքնակալների մէջ, իբրեւ պայմանի փոխադարձ սիրոյ եւ օգնականութեան, որը պետք է մնար անխախտ սերունդից սերունդ: Այդ դաշնադրութիւնը պահպանվեցաւ Տրդատի ամբողջ կենդանութեան ժամանակ եւ Հայաստանը մի ամուր պատնէշ դարձաւ պարսիկների դէմ, թոյլ չտալով նրանց յարձակվել Հռովմէական Կայսրութեան սահմանների վրա:

«Տրդատը ահարկու սուր էր մեր հայրենիքի թշնամիների դէմ, եւ իր թագաւորութեան բոլոր ժամանակը սարսափի մէջ էր պահում ամբողջ Պարսկաստանը եւ նրանց Շապուհ թագաւորին: Նա մեռաւ եւ մեր աշխարհը անմխիթար սուգի մէջ թողեց:

«Հայաստանը այժմ ալեկոծվում է անիշխանութեան մէջ: Նախարարների մէջ տիրում է երկպառակութիւն եւ ներքին պատերազմ: Սանատրուկը ինքնագլուխ թագաւոր է դարձել Փայտակարանում: Նախարարներից ոմանք, նրա օրինակին հետեւելով, իրաքանչիւրը ձգտում է իր իշխանութեան թագաւորը լինել: Աղձնեաց Բակուր բդեշխը ապստամբված է հայոց նախարարների միաբանութիւնից եւ նոյն նպատակին է հետեւում: Թշնամին, օգուտ քաղելով ներքին խռովութիւնից, ամէն կողմից ներում է մեզ: Շապուհը, հին վրէժխնդրութեան ծարաւը հագեցընելու համար, կատաղի գազանի նման, մեր երկիրը աւերակ է դարձնում: Հայաստանի գահը թափուր է մնացած իր հարազատ արքայից: Մի

մեծ, մի գլխաւոր չը կայ, որ ի մի հաւաքէ բոլոր անջատուած ուժերը եւ ընդհանուր զօրու-
թեամբ դէմ դնէ թշնամուն: Հայաստանը քայ-
քայման վիճակի մէջ է: Ձեր մի խօսքը բաւական
է մեր աշխարհը օրհասական վտանգից ազատելու համար: Ի սէր ազգի, ի սէր հայրենիքի, բա-
րեխօսեցէք կայսրի մօտ, յիշեցրէք նրան մեր հին
դաշնակրութիւնը, եւ նրա օգնութիւնը խնդրե-
ցէք՝ Տրդատի որդի Խոսրովին հօր տեղը թագաւոր դնելու: Դրանով դուք կատարած կը լինէք
ձեր սուրբ պարտաւորութիւնը դէպի ձեր անբախտ հայրենիքը եւ դէպի այն ազգը, որ պարծենում է ձեզանով եւ իրան մեծ պատիւ է համարում ձեզ իր որդի կոչելու:

«Բացի այդ նամակից, առանձին թուղթ
գրվեցաւ մեր եւ նախարարների կողմից կայսրին
մատուցանելու համար, եւ արքայավայել ընծա-
ներով ուղարկվեցաւ տեղդ՝ Ծոփաց Մար իշխանի եւ Հաշտենից Գազ իշխանի ձեռքով: Այդ իշխանները բերանացի կը պատմեն ձեզ, ինչ որ
պակաս ենք թողել մեր նամակի մէջ»:[21]

Ոչ մի ջիղ ոչ մի մկնակ չը շարժվեցաւ հրա-
ւետորի սառն դէմքի վրա այդ ողբալի նամակի

---

21 «Ուստի ուշ ի կուրծս անկեալ եւ ի միտս եկեալ նախարարցն
հայոց. Ժողովեցան առ մեծն վրթանէս, եւ առաքեցին երկուս
ի պատուաւոր իշխանացն. զՄար իշխանն Ծոփաց, եւ զԳազ
իշխանն Հաշտենից, երթալ ի նախազահի քաղաքն առ կայսրն
Կոստանդոս՝ որդի Կոստանդիանոսի, հանդերձ պատարագաւ
եւ թղթով:» —Խորենացի

ընթերցանութեան ժամանակ: Նա մի կողմ դրեց նամակը եւ մտածութեան մէջ ընկաւ, որպէս մի մարդ, որ գտնվում է անել դրութեան մէջ:

—Դուք դեռ չէ՞ք ներկայացել կայսրին,—հարցրեց նա, դառնալով դէպի երկու իշխանները:

—Ոչ, չր նայելով որ այդ մասին բազմիցս խնդրած ենք պալատականներից,—պատասխանեցին նրանք:

—Իսկ կայսրին յայտնի՞ է ձեր գալուստը:

—Հարկաւ պէտք է յայտնի լինի. մենք դատարկաձեռն չէինք եկած, մենք բերել էինք մեզ հետ արքայավայել ընձաներ. մեր ընձաները ցոյց են տուել կայսրին: Այդ մասին ձեզ եւս գրել է մեր Վրթանէս հայրապետը:

—Այո՛, գրել է... Իսկ այժմ ինչո՞ւմն է դժուարութիւնը:

—Իսկապէս ոչինչում,—պատասխանեց Հաշտենից իշխանը:—Ի՞նչ դժուարութիւն պիտի կրենք, երբ մենք ունենք կայսրի պալատում մի ձեզ պէս յարգված անձն: Բաւական է ձեր մի խոսքը եւ կայսրը կը կատարէ մեր խնդիրքը: Այժմ ձեզանից է կախված մեր պատգամաւորութեան յաջողութիւնը:

—Ինձանի՞ց... հարցրեց հռետորը շփոթվելով:—Բայց ես չր գիտեմ, թէ ո՛րքան յարմար կը լինի իմ միջամտութիւնը...

Երկու իշխանները մնացին զարմացած. նրանք այսպիսի պատասխանի չէին սպասում:

—Ինչո՞ւմն է ձեր տարակուսանքը,—հարցրեց Ծովաց իշխանը:

—Նրանում, որ ես քաղաքականութեամբ չեմ զբաղվում, ինձ բոլորովին յայտնի չէ, թէ կայսրը ի՞նչ հայեացք կամ նպատակներ ունի Հայաստանի թագաւորութեան մասին:

Ծովաց իշխանը, որ աւելի դիւրագրգիռ էր, քան թէ իր ընկերը, բաւական զայրացած կերպով ասաց.

—Կայսրի նպատակները կարող են լինել՝ կամ ի նպաստ, կամ աննպաստ Հայաստանին. այսինքն նա կամ կը ցանկանայ, որ Հայաստանի թագաւորութիւնը պահպանվի, կամ կը ցանկա- նայ, որ ոչնչանա եւ Հայաստանը Հռովմէական Կայսրութեան մի նահանգ դառնայ: Ասացէք, խնդրեմ, դուք ի՞նչպէս կը վարվէիք, եթէ կայսրի նպատակը այդ վերջինը լինէր:

—Ես կը թողնէի նրա կամքին:

—Իսկ եթէ կայսրը ցանկանո՞ւմ է, որ պահպանվի Հայաստանը:

—Այն ժամանակ ես կը միջամտէի:

—Որքան գովելի է ձեր անկեղծ խոստուա- նութիւնը,—մէջ մտաւ Հաշտենից իշխանը,—այն- քան էլ պախարակելի է ձեր հաճոյամոլութիւնը կայսրին։ Եթէ այսպէս խօսէր մի հռովմայեցի, ես կը գովէի նրա հայրենասիրութիւնը։ Եթէ հռովմայեցին ասեր ինձ. ես կը նայեմ իմ կայսրի ցանկութեանը, եթէ նա կամենում է, որ Հայաստանը միանայ Կայսրութեան հետ, այն ժամանակ ես էլ նոյնը կը ցանկանամ։ Իսկ եթէ կայսրը ցանկանում է, որ Հայաստանը պահպանվի, ես էլ կը ցանկանամ, որ պահպանվի։ Հռովմայեցու մի այսպիսի դատողութիւնը ինձ չէր բարկացնի։ Բայց երբ այսպէս խօսում է մի հայ, նա կորցնում է իմ աչքում իր բոլոր նշանակութիւնը, որքան էլ բարձր լինէր նա։

Հռետորը ամէնեին չլիրավորվեցաւ այդ կծու խօսքերից. նա չափազանց ներողամիտ մարդ էր։ Նրա սառն դէմքի վրա, կարծես կարդացվում էին այդ խօսքերը. «իզուր էք բարկանում, իշխան, ես ինչո՞վ եմ մեղաւոր, որ դժբախտութիւն եմ ունեցել հայ ծնվելու»... Բայց այդ խօսքերը չասաց նա, այլ խիստ մեղմութիւնով պատասխանեց.

—Դուք բոլորովին սխալ հասկացաք իմ ասածը, իշխան, ես աւելի մեծ վատահութիւնով կը բարեխոսէի կայսրի մօտ Հայաստանի համար, եթէ հռովմայեցի լինէի։ Բայց իմ հայութիւնը իմ լեզուն կաշկանդում է։ Ես չեմ ցանկանում ներբան դժուարին դրութեան մէջ դնել, թէեւ ես հաստատ գիտեմ, ինչ որ խնդրելու լինեմ, նա չի մերժի։ Բայց ես սովորութիւն չեմ ունեցել խնդրել

նրանից այն բանը, որ ամենափոքր դժկամու-
թիւն կարող էր պատճառել նրան։ Ես ինձ թոյլ
չեմ տայ դէպի չարը գործ դնել կայսրի իմ վերա-
բերութեամբ ունեցած հաւատն ու սէրը։

—Այդ իրաւացի կը լինէր, եթէ հարցը ձեր
անձին կամ ձեր մասնաւոր շահերին վերաբե-
րէր, բայց այստեղ հարցը վերաբերում է ձեր
հայրենիքի մահուան եւ կեանքի խնդրին,—նկատեց Հաշտենից իշխանը։

—Հէնց այդ է, որ ինձ դժուարութեան մէջ
է դնում,—պատասխանեց հռետորը մի առանձին
բաւականութեամբ, որպէս թէ, վիճաբանութեան
խնդիրը արդէն լուծուեցաւ։—Իմ հայրենիքը ա-
ւելի մօտ է իմ անձին, քան թէ մի օտար երկիր։
Իմ շահերը աւելի կապուած են իմ հայրենիքի
հետ, քան թէ մի օտար երկրի հետ։ այստեղից
այն պարզ եզրակացութեանը կը հասնենք, որ
խնդրելով իմ հայրենիքի համար, միեւնոյն է, որ
ես կը խնդրէի իմ անձի համար։ Բայց ես իմ անձ-
նական շահերի համար խնդրելու սովորութիւն
չունեմ։ Աւելի մեծ յօժարութեամբ կը միջամտէի
ես, եթէ Հայաստանը մի օտար երկիր լինէր։

Երկու իշխաններն եւս զայրացած կերպով
ոտքի ելան։

—Մեր խօսակցութիւնը վերջացած է,—ասա-
ցին նրանք։—Այժմ ամէն ինչ մեզ համար պարզ է։
Դուք վերին աստիճանի եսական էք, Պարոյր։

Դուք չէք ցանկանում ձեր անձասիրութիւնը զոհել հայրենիքի փրկութեան համար: Դուք վախենում էք կայսրի աչքում հայրենասէր երեւալ, որովհետեւ այդ կարող էր կասկածանքի ենթարկել ձեր անձը: Բայց իմացած եղէք, Պարոյր, եթէ ինքը կայսրը հոռվմայեցոյ սիրտ ունի, նա կը յարգէ հայրենասիրութիւնը ամեն մի անհատի մէջ: Նա վա՛տ, ցա՛ծ եւ փոքրոգի՛ կը համարի այն մարդուն, որ դէպի իր հայրենիքի դժբախտութիւնը սառնասիրտ է մնում...

Երկու իշխանները հեռացան:

Հռետորի դէմքի վրա երեւաց մի բարեսիրտ ժպիտ, նման այն ժպիտներին, որ երեւում է չափահաս, զարգացած մարդկանց դէմքի վրա, երբ լսում են մի երեխայի դատողութիւնները:

«Պարգամի՛տ մարդիկ,—ասաց նա իշխանների հեռանալուց յետոյ,—ամեն մի բնական հայրենասիրութիւնը ներելի է համարում միայն իր եւ իր համացեղ հպատակների համար, իսկ դէպի օտարի հայրենասիրութիւնը անհամբեր է լինում»...

Միւս օրը հռետորը պէտք է թողներ Հռոմվմը: Նա պատրաստվեցաւ ներկայանալ կայսրին եւ իր վերջին հրաժարական ողջոյնը մատուցանել: Մի խումբ պալատական աստիճանաւորներ նրան առաջնորդում էին դէպի արքունիքը: Կայսրը ընդունեց նրան խորին խնդակցութեամբ, եւ միեւնոյն ժամանակ իր ապ ոսանքը արտայայտելով, որ գրկվում է իր սիրելի ճիւրի ախորժելի հասարակութիւնից:

—Շնորհակալ եմ քեզանից, Պրոյերեսիոս, ասաց աշխարհի վեհապետը, ձեռք տալով նըր-ան,—քո ներկայութեամբ իմ պալատում՝ դու քաղցրացրիր իմ բազմահոգ ժամերը, իսկ քո ի-մաստութեամբ իմ քաղաքում՝ դու բարձրացրիր ճարտասանական ամբիօնը: Քաղաքը կատարեց իր շնորհակալութեան պարտքը եւ քո անունով արձան կանգնեցրեց: Մնում եմ ես: Խնդրի՛ր ինձանից, ինչ որ քո ցանկութիւնն է: Ես պատ-րաստ եմ կատարել:

Խիստ բարեպատեհ առիթ ունէր Պարոյրը, կայսրի այդ առաջարկութիւնից յետոյ, բարեխօ-սել իր հայրենիքի մասին, եւ խնդրել այն, ինչ որ նրանից պահանջում էին: Նա լիշեց այդ, բայց տատանվեցաւ անվճռականութեան մէջ...

—Պրոյերեսիոսը այդ անշուք վերարկուն հագել է, որ խնդրելու ոչինչ չունենայ այդ աշ-խարհում,—պատասխանեց հպարտ իմաստասէ-րը:

Երբ կայսրը երկար թախանձեց նրան, նա ասաց.

—Աթէնքը, այդ իմաստութեան քաղաքը, պարգեւեց ինձ մտաւոր սնունդ: Բոլորը, ինչ որ ունեմ ես, այդ քաղաքին եմ պարտական: Ես կը ցանկանայի դիւրացնել աթենացոց մարմնական սնունդը:

Յետոյ նկարագրեց նա քաղաքի մէջ տիրող աղքատութիւնը, ունեստների թանկութիւնը, որը աւելի ծանրանում է մաքսերի չափազանցութեամբ, եւ վերջապէս, խնդրեց, որ քաղաքը մտնող բոլոր ունեստները, թէ ալիւր, թէ ցորեան եւ թէ այլ պաշարեղէններ, բոլորը ազատ լինեն մաքսից: Երիտասարդական հասակում, Աթէնքի ամենաաղքատ թաղերից մէկում բնակւած լինելով, հռետորի մէջ խիստ տխուր յիշողութիւններ էին մնացել քաղաքացիների թշուառութեան մասին:

—Ձեր խնդիրքը շատ համեստ է, բայց առաքինական է,—ասաց կայսրը:—Թող լինի այդպէս, որպէս ցանկանում էք:

Աթէնքի Անատոլիոս եպարքոսին հրաման գրւեցաւ, որ վերացնեն մաքսերը:

Հռետորը թողեց Հռովմը եւ ուղեւորւեցաւ դէպի Աթէնք: Հասնելով այնտեղ, կատարեց հռովմայեցիների խնդիրքը եւ իր աշակերտներից մէկին, Եւսեփիոս աղէքսանդրացուն, ուղարկեց Հռովմ, որ իր փոխարէն իմաստասիրական եւ ճարտասանական դասեր կարդայ:

Հայոց երկու իշխանները հասան նոյնպէս իրանց նպատակին: Թէեւ Պարոյրը զլացաւ նրանց մի խօսքով անգամ օգնել, եւ աւելի բարւոք համարեց Աթէնքի աղքատների հացի համար հոգ տանել, քան թէ ամբողջ Հայաստանը ազատել կործանումից,—բայց հայոց մեծահոգի իշ-

խաննները, արհամարհելով հայրենիքի խորթացած որդու օտարամոլությունը, իրանք անձամբ
դիմեցին կայսրին, եւ մատուցանելով սուրբ Վրըթանէս հայրապետի ու նախարարների թուղթը,
սիրալիր ընդունելություն գտան: Կայսրը կատարեց նրանց խնդիրքը, եւ Անտիոքոս զորապետին
զորքով ուղարկեց Հայաստան, որը զալով՝ խաղաղությունը վերականգնեց, եւ Տրդատի որդի
Խոսրովը իր հօր տեղը հայոց գահը բարձրացաւ:

Պարոյրի կատարած բարեխոսությունը, մաքսերի բարձման վերաբերությամբ, աւելի բարձրացրեց նրա հարգը աթենացոց աչքում: Մեծ շրնորհակալությեամբ ընդունեցին նրան եւ կրկին
յանձնեցին նրա բաց թողած ճարտասանական
ամբիօնը: Այդ ամբիօնը սիրում էր նա, աւելի քան
մի կայար, որ սիրում է իր գահը: Այդ ամբիօնից
իշխում էր նա մտքերի, սրտերի եւ հոգիների
վրա: Այդ ամբիօնին նուիրված էր նա իր հոգու
բոլոր զգացմունքներով: Եւ շպէտք է զարմանալ
եւ ոչ մեղադրել նրան, որ նա դէպի իր հայրենիքը
եւ դէպի նրա հոգսերը անտարբեր էր: Նա գիտութեան եւ իմաստութեան սիրահար էր: Այդ սէրը
մոռանալ էր տուել նրան ուրիշ բոլոր սէրերը:

Աթէնքի ճարտասանական ամբիօնը կառավարեց նա մինչեւ Յուլիանոսի ինքնակալ ընտրվելու օրերը: Այդ քրիստոնէչւթիւնը հալածող եւ
հեթանոսական իմաստակներին հովանաւորող
կայսրը, որը բոլոր դպրոցներից հեռացրեց

քրիստոնեայ իմաստասէրներին եւ նրանց փոխարէն հեթանոսներ նշանակեց,—այդ ուրացողը Պարոյրին չլիկաւ, նրան թողեց իր տեղում: Յուլիանոսը, որ իրան եւս մեծ իմաստասէր էր համարում, բայց դարձեալ Պարոյրի գիտութեան ու հանճարի մասին խորին ակնածութիւն ունէր: Նա անձամբ ծանօթ էր հռետորի հետ, նրա հետ թղթակցում էր, եւ իր նամակներից մէկի մէջ կոչում էր նրան. «Պերիկլէսի համանման, յորդարատ եւ անարգել զետ պերճախոսութեան»:

Յուլիանոսը մի առանձին ակնկալութիւն եւս ունէր հռետորից. նա ցանկանում էր, որ Պարոյրը գրէ նրա զինուորական գործողութիւնների պատմութիւնը: Նա փափագում էր՝ երեւելի հռետորի ճարտար գրչով անմահացնել իր անունը: Բայց ազնիւ հռետորը, որ բնաւ շողոքորթութեան սովորած չէր, մերժեց նրա խնդիրքը ասելով, «իմ ձեռքը չի գրի Քրիստոսի վարդապետութիւնը հալածող մի կայսրի պատմութիւնը»: Այդ մերժումից յետոյ, հռետորը իր յօժարութեամբ թողեց Աթէնքի ճարտասանական ամբիոնը, չը կամենալով իր դիրքով պարտաւորուած մնալ կայսրին:

Նրա բազմաթիւ աշակերտների թւում նրշանաւոր եղան՝ մեծն Բարսեղ, Կեսարիայի պատրիարքական աթոռի պարծանքը եւ սուրբ Գրիգոր աստուածաբանը, որ իր ստուար աշխատութիւններով յայտնի է յունական մատենագրութեան մէջ: Այդ վերջինի գրչին է պատկանում այն բանաստեղծութիւնը, որ դրած է այդ գլխի ճակատին: Նրա աշակերտներից մէկն էր նաեւ երիտասարդ Եւնաքիսոը, որ գրեց իր սիրելի վարժապետի կենսագրութիւնը:

Իբրեւ մարդ, Պարոյրը կեանքի քթոյշ կողմերից եւս զուրկ չմնաց: Փոքր Ասիայի Տրալլի քաղաքում զտնված ժամանակ, սիրահարվեցաւ Ամֆիկլեա անունով մի յոյն օրիորդի վրա, որի հետ եւ ամուսնացաւ նա: Այդ ամուսնութիւնից ունեցաւ երկու դուստր, որոնց յոյն փեսաների տալուց յետոյ, իր ազատութիւնը ընտանեկան կեանքով չկաշկանդելու համար, սկեց կնոջից բաժանված ապրել:

Պարոյրը խորին ծերութեան հասաւ, նա մեռաւ 95 տարեկան հասակում: Առաքինութիւնը, անարատութիւնը նրա պատուաւոր կեանքի յատկանիշներն էին: Իսկ տոկուն եւ եռանդուն աշխատութիւնը նրա անվաստակելի հոգու մեծ զօրութիւնն էր: Յունաց գրքերի մէջ նա փառա֊ ւոր անուն թողեց: Ապէնքը պարծենում էր նրա֊ նով, իսկ Հռովմը նրա պատուի համար արձան կանգնեց: Իսկ այդ մեծ հռետորը հայ մարդու սրտում մի փոքրիկ տեղ անգամ չգտաւ: Մեր մա֊ տենագիրներից ոչ ոք չէ խոսում նրա մասին: Նա ապրեց, գործեց գիտութեան եւ իմաստու֊ թեան համար, բայց իր հայրենիքի համար կո֊ րած մարդ էր...

Նա, իրաւ է, փառաւոր տեղ բռնեց այն մեծ մարդկանց անունների շարքում, որոնց ստեղծել է յունաց պատմութիւնը, բայց անունների այդ երկայն շարքի մէջ նրա փայլը, միախառնուելով միւս շատերի լոյսի հետ, անհետացաւ... Բայց եթէ իր հայրենիքում գործէր, նա առաջինը կը լինէր, նա եզականը կը լինէր, եւ նրա յիշատակը յաւիտեան չէր մոռացվի...

ԳԼՈՒԽ Ե

«Երանելի փիլիսոփան Մովսէս [Խորենացի], որ արդարեւ մինչդեռ էր ի մարմնի՝ ցանկ երկնային զօրացն էր քաղաքակից. ո՞չ ապաքէն ի տեղւոջէ ի տեղի
աբեղեանդ հայոց հալածական արարին։
Ո՞չ զլուսաւորիչն եւ զոգիտահալած զգրեանն նորա առ անգիտութեան «փաթառիկես» կոչին. եւ այլ բազում ինչ իրոք
թշնամանեալ յետոյ՝ ապա յաղագս այլոց
ամօթոյ՝ գխափելական գեւխսկոպոսութիւնս նման դեղոց մահու արբուցեալ
Սրբոյն՝ հեղձուցին... Զոսկերան [Խորենացւոյ] ի գերեզմանէն հանել տային [աբեղեանն հայոց] եւ զետ արկանել. Զհրպեշտականնման այրն զՏէր նոյն՝ անհանգիստ հալածանօք վախճանեցուցին, որք
եւ այժմ դեռեւս անյագութեամբ քինով ընդ
մեռելոյն կացին»։

—Ղազար Փարպեցի

Աշնան փոթորկալի գիշերներից մէկն էր։ Կատադի քամին մունչելով պտտվում էր շինականների
գեւնապիոր խրճիթների վրա եւ ցրիւ էր տալիս
խոտի դեզերը, որ կիտած էին կտուրների վրա։
Երկինքը ամպամած էր, խաւարը տիրում էր ամեն

տեղ: Բացի քամու աղմուկից, ուրիշ ձայն չէր լսվում: Շներն անգամ այն գիշեր փախել, մտել էին իրանց ծակերը, եւ մի առանձին երկչոտութեամբ սպասում էին, կարծես, աշխարհի կատարածին:

Դա Տարօն գաւառի Խնորնի գիւղն էր, որի փոքրիկ խրճիթներից մէկում իւղային ճրագը դեռ մարած չէր: Այդ գետնափոր, ստորերկրեայ բնակարանի խորշերից մէկում նստած էր մի ծերունի: Քամին երբեմն ուժեղ հոսանքով ներս էր փչում երդիքից, եւ ճրագի լոյսը ծածանվելով, տալիս էր ծերունու ալեզարդ դէմքին խորհրդաւոր կերպարանք: Նա միայնակ էր: Նրա շուրջը, նոյն կոշտ օթոցի վրա, ուր նստած էր նա, անկանոն կերպով դրած էին զանազան հին գրքեր յունարէն, պարսկերէն եւ ասորերէն լեզուով: Նա այն աստիճան խորասուզված էր այդ հին մագաղաթների մէջ, որ ամենեւին չէր նկատում, թէ ի՛նչ էր կատարվում դրսում: Դրանք էին նրա մտերիմ ընկերները, դրանք էին նրա հաւատարիմ խորհրդակիցները, սկսեալ այն օրից, երբ նա ամեն տեղից հալածված, այդ ողորմելի խրճիթում վարում էր տխուր, առանձնական կեանք:

Խրճիթը աւելի գերեզմանի էր նման, քան թէ կենդանի մարդու բնակարանի: Դա բնակութեան այն նախնական ձեւն էր, երբ մարդիկ իրանց կենցաղավարութեան եղանակներով շատ չէին տարբերվում վայրենի գազաններից: Դա կատարեալ որչ էր։ Ցերեկով անգամ մի բան պարզ տեսնելու համար հարկաւոր էր այնտեղ ճրագ վառել։ Բորբոսային անշարժ օդը խեղդելու չափ ծանր էր։ Պատերը նոյնպես ծածկւած էին բորբոսային կանաչութեամբ։ Խոնաւութիւնը տիրում էր ամեն տեղ։ Որ կողմ էլ շօշափում էիր, փուլ էր գալիս, հոդ էր թափվում։ Քարերն անգամ փտել, հողմահարվել էին մշտապես տիրող խոնաւութիւնից։ Իսկ ծերունի աշխատաւորը ապրում էր այդ մռայլ գերեզմանի մէջ,—ապրում էր, պատերազմելով իր սպանիչ մթնոլորտի լուծանող, քայքայող եւ չլատող ազդեցութեան հետ։

Այդ մթին գերեզմանի մէջ երջանիկ էր նա։ Երջանիկ էր իր դառն անբախտութեան մէջ։ Այստեղ նրան չէին խանգարում. այստեղ նա մոռացված էր թէ աշխարհից եւ թէ իր բազմաթիւ թշնամիներից։ Այդքանն էլ բաւական էր նրան, որ գոնէ ժամանակ էր գտնում իրագործելու այն բարձր նպատակը, որի մեծութեան առջեւ անզգալի էին դարձել կեանքի բոլոր վշտերը, որը ձգել էր նրան այդ սոսկալի անձնուրացութեան մէջ։ Աղքատութիւնը, անօթութիւնը եւ տառապանքը անբաժան էին նրանից,—անբաժան էին եւ այն մազաղաբթները, որոնցով շրջապատել էր իրան, որոնց մէջ գտնում էր իր արտի միակ մխիթարութիւնը։

Ծերունին Մովսէս Խորենացին էր։ Այդ խրճիթի տատապանքների մէջ գրեց նա իր հրաշալի պատմութիւնը, որպէս Իսրայէլի Մովսէսը, առանձնացած Սինայեան լեռան կայծակների եւ որոտման մէջ, քարեայ տախտակների վրա գրծում էր Աստուածային պատգամները։

Դրսում փոթորիկը չէր դադարել։ Ծերունին դեռ շարունակում էր պարապել։ Այդ միջոցին լսելի եղաւ խրճիթի դռան մելամաղձային ճռոցը։ Ուշիկ քայլերով ներս մտաւ մի մանկահասակ աղջիկ։ Տեսնելով ծերունու զբաղմունքը, նա կամենում էր նոյնպէս աննկատելի կերպով դուրս գալ, որպէս մտել էր։ Բայց ծերունին գլլուխը վեր բարձրացրեց եւ, նայելով նրա վրա, ասաց.

—Ի՞նչ կայ, Շուշանիկ։

—Եկայ քնելու տեղդ շտկելու, հայրիկ։

—Ես դեռ պիտի նստեմ, դու գնա քնի՛ր, զաւակս։

Շուշանիկը ծերունու այրի մնացած քրոջ դուստրն էր։ Նոյն խրճիթի մէջն էր բնակվում նրա մայրը, որ բաժանում էր իր եղբոր դառն աղքատութիւնը։ Մայրը վրանններ եւ կապերտներ էր գործում եւ իր ձեռքի վաստակով պահում էր եղբօրը։ Իսկ աղջիկը սպասաւորում էր նրան։

Չը նայելով, որ ծերունին իրաւունք տուեց նրան չը սպասել իրան, այլ գնալ եւ հանգստանալ, բայց Շուշանիկը դարձեալ սկսեց պատրաստել նրա անշուք անկողինը։ Նոյն կոշտ մագզ օթոցի մի կողմում, որի վրա նստած էր ծերունին, դրեց նրա բարձը, լեցրած չոր խոտով, եւ նոյնպէս կոշտ մագից գործված վերմակը տարածելուց յետոյ, իր ամենօրեայ սովորութեան համեմատ, մի առանձին քնքշութեամբ մոտեցաւ մօրեղբօրը բարի գիշեր ասելու։ Ծերունին գրկեց նրան եւ օրհնելով համբուրեց։ Ընտանեկան սէրը դեռ չէր հանգել նրա խորտակված սրտում։ Այդ նազելի աղջիկը նոյնքան սիրելի էր նրան, որքան նրա բարեսիրտ մայրը։

Այդ միջոցին խարճթի դուռը դրսից սկսեցին սաստիկ բախել։

—Երեւի, քամին է,—ասաց ծերունին։

—Ոչ, քամին չէ,—պատասխանեց Շուշանիկը, եւ դուրս վազեց տեսնելու, թէ ո՞վ է այդ տարաժամ հիւրը։

Մի քանի րոպէից յետոյ Շուշանիկը ուրախութեամբ ներս մտաւ, ասելով.

—Յուսիկն է, հայրիկ։

—Յուսի՞կը,—զարմացած կերպով կրկնեց ծերունին։—Ի՞նչ կայ, ի՞նչու է եկել։

—Նա թրջված է. դրսում անձրեւ է գալիս, մտաւ մորս մոտ հագուստը ցամաքացնելու, շուտով ձեզ մոտ կը գայ,—պատասխանեց Շուշանիկը առանց ծերունու հարցերի վրա ուշադրութիւն դարձնելու։

Յուսիկը մի երիտասարդ աբեղայ էր, սուրբ

Կարապետի վանքի միաբան, եւ մանկութիւնից աշակերտած լինելով ծերունու մօտ, այնքան սիրում էր իր վարժապետին, որպէս իր հարազատ հօրը։ Նրա գալուստը թէեւ անչափ ուրախութիւն պատճառեց ծերունուն, բայց, միւս կողմից, նա սաստիկ մտատանջութեան մէջ ընկաւ, թէ ի՞նչ էր նշանակում այդ անակնկալ յայտնվելը, այն էլ մի այնպիսի փոթորկային եւ վտանգաւոր ժամանակում։

Նրա մտատանջութիւնը աւելի սաստկացաւ, երբ երիտասարդ աբեղան մտաւ նրա մօտ աշխարհականի հագուստով։

— Այդ ի՞նչ է նշանակում,— բացականչեց ծերունին զարհուրելով,— ի՞նչու ես կերպարանափոխ եղել, այլեւս ո՞ր դժբախտ պատահարը քեզ այստեղ բերեց, գիշերվայ այդ ժամուն, եղանակի այդ խստութեան ժամանակ։

— Հանգստացէք, հայրիկ,— պատասխանեց երիտասարդ աբեղան մօտենալով եւ նրա օրհնութիւնն առնելով,— չար ոչինչ չէ պատահել, ես իսկոյն բոլորը կը պատմեմ ձեզ։

Նա նստեց ծերունուց փոքր ինչ հեռու։ Նրա խօսքերից երեւաց, թէ հիւանդ եղբայր ունի մերձակայ գիւղում, վանահօրից թոյլտուութիւն խնդրելով, եկած էր եղբօրը տեսնելու, եւ այդ դէպքից օգուտ քաղելով, մտածեց այցելել իր վարժապետին։ Իսկ գիշերով գալու եւ հագուստ փոխելու պատճառը այն է, որ իրան, վարժա-

պետին յայտնի պետք է լինի, որ նրա մոտ մոտ մեռ-
նողների վրա միւս հոգեւորականները կասկածանքով են նայում:

Նրա պատմութեան առաջին մասը բոլորովին շինծու էր. նա ոչ հիւանդ եղբայր ունէր
եւ ոչ գնացել էր նրան տեսնելու: Նա ուղիղ ե-
կած էր ծերունու մոտ, բայց թէ ի՞նչ նպատակով,—այդ մասին զգուշութեամբ լռեց, չկամենա-
լով միանգամից հարուածել նրա առանց դրան էլ
խորտակուած սիրտը:

Ծերունին փոքրինչ հանգստացաւ:

—Այո՛, ինձ յայտնի է,—ասաց նա մի առանձին դառնութեամբ,—որ ինձ մոտ մտնողների
վրա կասկածանքով են նայում հայոց աբեղաները, աղանդաւոր են համարում... Պատմեցէք,—
խօսքը փոխեց նա—ի՞նչ նորութիւններ կան ձեր
վանքում:

Երիտասարդը սկսեց պատմել զանազան
վանական ինտրիգների մասին, աբեղաների ծու-
լութեան եւ զոշաքաղութեան մասին: Ծերունին
անհետաքրքրութեամբ լսում էր, որպէս մի սովո-
րական բան, եւ գլուխը քարշ ձգած, առանց
երիտասարդի երեսին նայելու, իր շուրջը ընկած
գրքերը խնամքով վեր էր առնում եւ մի կողմ
էր դնում: Բոլորը հաւաքեց նա, բայց նրանցից
մէկը, որ ինքն էր գրել, պահեց իր ձեռքում: Երի-
տասարդին ծանօթ էր այդ գիրքը, նա հետա-
քրքրութեամբ հարցրեց.

—Դեռ չէ՞ք աւարտել, հայրիկ:

—Պատմութիւնը աւարտել եմ. այսօր գրեցի իմ ողբը. դա կը լինի իմ աշխատութեան վերջաբանը:

—Մի՞նչեւ ո՞րտեղ հասցրիք պատմութիւնը:

—Մինչեւ Արշակունեաց թագաւորութեան եւ մեր Լուսավորիչ նոր տոհմի Հայրապետական Աթոռի անկումը: Աւելի հեռու գնալ չէի կարող, որ նկարագրէի մեր այժմեան կողերի ամօթալի գործերը: Դուք գիտէք, որ առանց դրան եւս, նըրանք ո՞րքան կատաղած են իմ դէմ:

Երիտասարդը առեց ծերունու ձեռքից գիրքը, սկսեց թերթել, միայն գլուխների վերնագրերը կարդալով:

—Այպքանն էլ բաւական է,—ասաց նա մի առանձին գոհութեամբ:

—Ես ամփոփեցի այդ գրքի մէջ մեր նախնեաց գործերը իրանց լաւ եւ վատ կողմերով, նկարագրեցի մեր աշխարհի դաւաճանների չարագործութիւնները եւ հայրենասէրների անձնագոհութիւնները: Դա մի կտակարան է, որ ես թողնում եմ ապագայ սերունդին: Կանցնեն խաւարի եւ տգիտութեան դարերը, կը ծնուի լուսաւոր ժամանակ իր նոր զաւակներով: Նրանք այդ կտակարանի մէջ կը տեսնեն նախնեաց թէ գեղեցիկ եւ թէ տգեղ յիշատակները: Նրանք կը սկսեն քննել, կը սկսեն դատել հայրերի գործերը, եւ անցեալի սխալներից խրատվելով, եւ անցեալի լաւ օրինակներից խրախուսվելով, կը ստեղծեն մի նոր կեանք, աւելի հաստատուն, աւելի ապահով հիմքերի վրա: Նրանք օգուտ կը քաղեն անցեալի փորձերից, կաշխատեն չզլորվել այն կորստեան վիհի մէջ, ուր հայերը անմտութեամբ ընկան...

—Եւ ձեր անունը կանմահանայ, որ թողնում էք ապագայի համար մի այնպիսի հայելի, որի մէջ գալոց սերունդը կը տեսնէ անցեալի տրխուր յիշատակները,—կը տեսնէ իր նախահարց մեծութիւնը եւ նրանց ցաւալի անկումը...—ընդհատեց երիտասարդը ծերունու խոսքը:

—Իմ անմահութեան վրա երբէք չեմ մտածել ես,—պատասխանեց ծերունին անկեղծ համեստութեամբ:—Ես աշխատել եմ անմահացնել մեր հայրենիքի յիշատակները, որ դրանք չմեռնեն, չը մոռացվին ազգի մտքից: Ոչինչ դրութիւն այնքան ցաւալի չէ երբ մի ազգ չը գիտէ իր նախնեաց պատմութիւնը: Դա միեւնոյն դժբախտ դրութեան նման կը լինի, երբ հայրը մեռնում է, իսկ իր անչափահաս ժառանգների համար չէ թողնում ոչ մի գրաւոր բան:

Երիտասարդ աբեղան ուշադրութեամբ լըսում էր. նրա խելացի դէմքը արտայայտում էր մի առանձին անհանգստութիւն: Կարծես, նա լռութեամբ ասում լինէր, «այդ բոլորը շատ գեղեցիկ է, շատ կրթողական է, բայց մենք այդ մասին դեռ երկար ժամանակ ունենք խոսելու, իսկ այժմ հարկաւոր է մի ամենակարեւոր հարցի մասին մտածել»:

— Դուք ձեր բնակարանը փոխելու դիտաւորութիւն չունե՞ք, հայրիկ,— ասաց նա, չկարողանալով այլ եւս համբերել:

— Ի՞նչ կայ,— հարցրեց ծերունին անհանգստութեամբ:

— Ոչինչ... այնպէս... հարցնում եմ...

— Երեւի, այստեղի՞ց եւս կամենում են հալածել ինձ...

— Ոչ... բայց... վատ չէր լինի՛ փոքր-ինչ զգոյշ լինել...

— Ո՞րտեղ փոխեմ, ո՞ւր գնամ,— պատասխանեց ծերունին դառնացած կերպով:— Կար ժամանակ, որ իմ ուժերը դեռ սպառուած չէին, աչքերումս լոյս կար եւ ոտներումս զօրութիւն: Թափառում էի մեր աշխարհի մի ծայրից միւսը, դիմանում էի քաղցի, ծարաւի եւ եղանակների խստութեանը: Իսկ այժմ ո՞ւր կարող եմ գնալ, ո՞րտեղ կարող եմ քարշ տալ այդ քայքայուած մեքենան:— Նա ձեռքը տարաւ դէպի իր անձը:— Իմ կեանքը անցաւ ցաւերով եւ դառնութեամբ. չմնաց մի տանջանք, որ ես կրած չլինէի: Իսկ այժմ, մի՞թէ այդ մխիթարութիւնից եւս կամենում են զրկել ինձ, եւ թոյլ չեն տալիս, որ գոնէ իմ ծերութեան վերջին օրերը անցկացնէի այդ խնձալ գերեզմանի մէջ:— Նա ցոյց տուեց իր կացարանը եւ րոպէական լռութիւնից յետոյ շաբունակեց աւելի դառնացած կերպով.

—Ես թողեցի, հետագայ նրանցից, սկսեցի առանձնութեան մէջ որոնել իմ սրտի հանգստութիւնը: Ես նրանց թողեցի հարուստ վանքերը եւ գաւառների շահաւէտ եպիսկոպոսութիւնները: Թող վայելեն, թող ուկի եւ արձաք դիզեն, որովհետեւ քաղցր է նրանց համար աշխարհի վայելչութիւնը: Ես նրանց չեմ խանգարում, եւ որքան էլ ցանկանայի, անկարող պիտի լինէի, որովհետեւ նրանք իրանց կողմն ունեն իրանց նման նախարարների ուժը եւ օտարի պաշտպանութիւնը, որ հայրենիքի շահերը վաճառելու գնով են ստանում: Այլեւս ի՞նչ են պահանջում ինձանից:Ինձ տուեցին Բագրեւանդի եպիսկոպոսութիւնը, միայն ինձ ծաղրելու համար, որ բարձրացնեն եւ այնտեղից ցած գլորեն, որպէս զի իմ կորձանումը աւելի զգալի լինի: Ես բոլորը տարայ, ամէն զրկանքի համբերեցի: Իմ կռիւը փառքի համար չէր: Ես պատերազմում էի խաւարի, տգիտութեան եւ հայրենիքի դաւաճանների դէմ: Ես յաղթվեցայ, ես ընկայ, եւ իմ կորձանման մէջն է իմ փառքը: Այժմ ի՞նչու չեն թողնում ինձ հանգչիլ իմ փլատակների վրա: Ես պատասպարվեցայ իմ հայրենական աղքատ տնակում: Ահա իմ բոլոր հարստութիւնը:—Նա ձեռքը մեկնեց դէպի իր մօտ դրած գրքերը:— Ես զրկվեցայ աշխարհից եւ մարդկային հասարակութիւնից, մի՞թէ չեն թողնելու, որ այդ լուռ,

անբարբառ մագաղաթների հետ խորհրդակցեմ
եւ նրանցով մխիթարեմ իմ դժբախտութեան
րոպէները: Ամէն ինչ խլեցին ինձանից,—մնաց մի
գրիչ միայն: Միթէ ա՞յդ եւս պիտի խլեն, որ անկարող լինեմ աւանդել իմ մտքերը, իմ սրտի
դառն զգացմունքները...

Վշտացած ծերունու բերանով խոսում էր
ժամանակի հալածված ճշմարտութիւնը:

—Պէտք է զգուշանալ աւելի վատթարից...
—պատասխանեց երիտասարդ աբեղան զգաց-
ված կերպով:—Այդ խաւարասէրները իրանց հա-
լածութեան մէջ չափ չունեն: Նրանք անդադար
նորանոր առիթներ են որոնում ձեզ հարուածե-
լու: Իսկ վերջին հարուածը ձեզ համար խիստ
կործտաբեր կը լինի...

—Մտածում են իրանց վաղեմի սովորութեան համեմատ թունավորե՞լ ինձ,—հարցրեց
ծերունին դառն արհամարհանքով:—Ես թոյնից
չեմ վախենում:

—Իրաւ է, չէք վախենում. այդ փորձը մի քանի անգամ արել են ձեզ հետ: Բայց...

—Այլ եւս ի՞նչ կարող են անել, բացի սպա-
նելուց: Դրանից աւելի դժուար վիճակ չէ կարող
լինել, որին ենթարկէին ինձ: Թող այդ ողորմելի
խրճիթից եւս արտաքսեն ինձ: Լեռների, ժայռե-
րի խոռոչներում կը գտնեմ մի այր պատսպար-
վելու համար: Մեր Լուսավորիչ հայրը, հալածված խաւարասէրների տգիտութիւնից, մի նոյն-

պիսի այրի մէջ մեռաւ: Իսկ ես նրա նուաստ աշակերտը լինելու արժանաւորութիւն չունեմ:

—Եթէ մինչեւ այստեղ հասներ հայածա- սերների վրէժխնդրութիւնը, դրանով եւս պէտք էր գոհ լինել: Բայց նրանց դիտաւորութիւնը աւելի չար է...

—Ասացէ՛ք, վերջապէս, մի՛ տանջէք ինձ: Ի՞նչ են կամենում անել:

—Նրանք մտածում են յափշտակել ձեր բո- լոր գրաւոր աշխատութիւնները եւ ոչնչացնել: Նրանք մտածում են ոչնչացնել այդ պատմու- թիւնը, որ ձեր վերջին տարիների ծանր վաս- տակների արգասիքն է: Ես հէնց այդ ցաւալի լուրը ձեզ հասցնելու համար, զադտնի կերպով դուրս եկայ վանքից, շտապեցի ձեզ մօտ, որ նա- խազգուշացնեմ:

—Անիրաւնե՛ր... գոչեց ծերունին խորին վրդովմունքով:—Ես ամեն ցածութիւններ կը սպասէի նրանցից, բայց այդ երեւակայել ան- գամ չէի կարող: Դա մի սարսափելի եղեռնա- գործութիւն է,—սպանել պատմութի՞ւնը: Դա ա- մենամեծն է բոլոր յանցանքներից: Նրանք կա- մենում են ոչնչացնել մեր նախնեաց գործերը եւ յաւիտենական մոռացութեան մէ՞ջ թաղել մեր հայրենիքի յիշատակները, որպէս զի իրանց վատ գործերն եւս նրանց հետ ծածկուեն, մոռացուեն եւ ապագայի համար ամօթի ու նախատինքի առարկայ չը դառնան:—Այո՛, դա կը լինէր ինձ

համար մահացու հարուած, եթէ նրանք հասնէ-
ին իրանց նպատակին: Այդ գիրքն էր մնացել
իմ վերջին մխիթարութիւնը, նրա մէջն էի ամփո-
փել իմ սիրտը, իմ հոգին, իմ բոլոր զգացմունքները: Նրա մէջն էի դրել իմ արտասուքը, որ թափել էի հայրենեաց աւերակների վրա...

Նա գլուխը քարշ ձգեց եւ ձեռքը տարաւ
դէպի ճակատը: Ալեւոր մազերը թափվեցան
պատկառելի ծերունու դէմքի վրա, եւ ծածկե-
ցին արտասուքը, որ հեղեղի նման հոսում էր նրա
աչքերից: Մի քանի րոպէ մնաց նա այդ թախծալի
դրութեան մէջ: Յետոյ շարունակեց աւելի գայ-
րացած կերպով:

—Ինձ չէ վշտացնում հանգամանքների
այդ դժբախտ հետեւանքը: Մեր ժամանակում
լոյսի եւ խաւարի կռիւը այլ կերպ չէր կարող
վերջանալ: Մեր Սահակ եւ Մեսրոպ հոր ա-
ռաջին աշակերտները պատերազմողների ա-
ռաջին դասակարգն էին: Նրանք ընկան: Նոյն
երանելի հարց կրտսեր աշակերտները—ես
եւ իմ ընկերները—պատերազմողի երկրորդ դասակարգն էինք: Մենք անցանք մեր նախորդ-
ների դիակների վրայով. թէեւ բաւական հեռու
գնացինք, բայց դարձեալ ընկանք: Մեր ուժերը
անհաւասար էին: Մենք պէտք է արմատախիլ
անէինք դարերով աճած, ստվարացած տգի-
տութիւնը, նախապաշարմունքը,—մենք պէտք է
սրբէինք ժողովրդի սրտից դարերով բարդուած,

թանձրացած բարոյական կեղտը։—Այդ հեշտ գործ չէր։ Մենք նոյնպէս պէտք է ընկնէինք, որպէս մեր նախորդները։ Մի քանի սերունդ պէտք է զոհվէր, մինչեւ նրանց դիակների վրայով ճանապարհ բացվէր դէպի լոյսը, դէպի ճշմարտութիւնը եւ դէպի բարին։—Իմ ընկերները այժմ միեւնոյն հալածանքների մէջն են, որպէս ես։ Մենք մեր անձերի վրա չենք մտածում։ Բայց ցաւալին այն կը լինէր, երբ մեր թըշնամիները կը յաջողեցնէին սպանել մեր գործը, մեր աշխատութիւնների արդիւնքը...

—Դեռեւս յուսահատվելու չէ, դեռեւս շատ ճնարներ կան ազատելու ձեր գրաւոր աշխատութիւննները,—պատասխանեց երիտասարդ աբեղան մի առանձին վստահութեամբ։—Այդ պատմութիւնը դուք գրել էք ձեր մեկենասի, Սահակ Բագրատունու, խնդիրքով։ Դուք դիտաւորութիւն ունէիք անձամբ տանել ձեր աշխատանքը եւ ձեր ձեռքով նուիրել ազնիւ իշխանին։ Այդ հասկացել են ձեր թշնամիները։ Նըրանք պատրաստվել են՝ կամ ձեր տան մէջ, կամ ճանապարհին կողոպտել ձեզ եւ յափշտակել այդ թանկագին գանձը։ Ժամանակ կորցնելու չէ։ Եթէ իմ բարի վարժապետր վստահութիւն ունի իր անձնանուէր աշակերտի վրա,—ես պատրաստ եմ հէնց այս գիշեր ճանապարհի ընկնել եւ տանել յանձնել իշխանին ձեր գիրքը։ Նրա ձեռքը հասնելուց յետոյ, ձեր աշխատութիւնը կազատվի վտանգից:

Ծերունին գրկեց իր մտերիմ աշակերտին եւ, օրհնելով նրան, ասաց.

— Դու միշտ բարի ես եղել եւ հակամէտ դէպի ճշմարիտը ու օգտակարը, Յուսիկ: Գովում եմ քո անձնանուիրութիւնը եւ մխիթարվում եմ, որովհետեւ դու ինքդ իմ աշխատութեան պրտուղներից մէկն ես: Եթէ քեզ նմանների թիւր շատ կը լինի, մեր յոյսերը պէտք է պսակված համարել: Մենք մեր գործը կատարեցինք, մեր վարը վարեցինք, մեր ցանքը ցանեցինք: Այսուհետեւ ձեզ է մնում մշակել, սնուցանել նորաբոյս ցանքը, որ փուշերը եւ տատասկները չխեղդեն նրան: Այսուհետեւ դուք եւ ձեր նմանները պէտք է լինեն մեր սկսած գործի շարունակողները: Օրհնում եմ քեզ, հաստատուն կամք, երանդ եւ զօրութիւն եմ խնդրում Ամենակալից: Տար այդ գիրքը եւ յանձնիր իշխանին: Նա միայն է, որ գիտէ գնահատել դրան, նա միայն է, որ հարգում է իր նախնեաց յիշատակները,—նա միայն է, որ ինձ հետ ցաւակից է եղել ներկայ թշուառութիւնների մէջ: Բագրատունիք միշտ հաւատարիմ են եղել դէպի հայրենեաց շահերը: Նա կը պահէ այդ գիրքը, որպէս մի սրբութիւն, եւ կառանդէ իր յաջորդներին: Հոգւոյ աչքով տեսնում եմ, որ մի օր Բագրատունիների տոհմիg պիտի կրկին ծագէ հայոց իշխանական գաւազանը: Եւ այն տոհմը, որ հայոց արքաների գլխին թագ էր դնում.—իր գլխին պիտի դնէ այդ թագը։ Իմ մարգարէութիւնները դու հաղորդիր իշխանին։

Գիրքը դրուեցաւ մի կաշեայ պարկի մէջ. երիտասարդ աբեղան կապեց մէջքի վրա, իսկ նրա վրայից հագաւ իր վերարկուն։ Յետոյ նա առեց իր ճանապարհորդական ցուպը եւ, համբուրելով ծերունու աջը, ուղի ընկաւ։

Դրսում փոթորիկը դեռ փոթորկւում էր. անձրեւը հեղեղի նման թափւում էր. սոսկալի քամին ժայռերը շարժում էր իրանց տեղից, բայց քաջասիրտ ուղեւորը հաստատուն քայլերով դիմում էր դէպի Սահակ Բագրատունու ամրոցը, որ մի քանի օրւայ ճանապարհով հեռու էր Խորենացու գիւղից։

—

Չանգահարութի՞ւն... տարաժամ զանգահարութի՞ւն... որ սոսկում է ազդում։ Ամէն կողմից լսելի էր լինում զանգակի ձանը, թախծալի հնչիւնը։ Նա լսելի էր լինում գիւղական փոքրիկ ժամատնից, լսելի էր լինում վանքերի բարձր զանգակատնից, լսելի էր լինում խուլ ձորերի եւ անբնակ լեռների մէջ առանձնացած, մեռաւոր մատուռներից։ Ամէն տեղ ղողանջում էր անսիրտ մեռաղը։ Մի չարագուշակ, հրաիրական ձայնով ղողանջում էր նա։

Դա այն ձայնը չէր, որ հրահրում է աղօթասէր շինականներին Աստուծոյ տաճարը՝ իրանց գոհութեան փառաբանութիւնը մատուցանելու Ամենակալին: Դա այն ձայնն էր, որ սարսափ է ազդում, որ գուշակում է մի որեւիցէ արհաւիրք, մի որեւիցէ տագնապ, մի որեւիցէ պատուհաս, որ վտանգ է սպառնում:

Օրը նոր էր լուսանում: Երկինքը խաղաղ էր. արեգակի պայծառ ճառագայթները ժպտում էին ցողազարդ դալարենիների հետ: Բնութիւնը հրճվում էր իր սքանչելի զեղեցկութեան մէջ: Նա, երեւի, չէր լսում զանգակների սոսկալի ձայնը եւ չէր վրդովվում:

Իսկ մարդիկ սաստիկ վրդովվմունքի մէջ էին: Ամէն ոք դուրս էր վազում իր բնակարանից, տեսնելու, թէ ի՞նչ էր պատահել: Խումբերով դուրս էին վազում սեւազգեստ աբեղաները, ոմանք վեղարով, ոմանք անվեղար, ոմանք ժամանակ չը գտնելով իրանց հողաթափերը հագնելու: Չարագուշակ ձայնը հասնում էր մինչեւ լեռնային քարանձաւի մէջ առանձնացած ճգնաւորի մենարանը, նա եւս թողնում էր իր մթին խորշը:

Շինականները դեռ նոր էին սկսել դաշտային աշխատութիւնները: Հանձաւորը թողնում էր հունձը եւ մանգաղը ձեռին գնում էր: Հերկողը թողնում էր իր արորն ու գութանը եւ խարազանը ձեռին վազ էր տալիս: Գիւղերից դուրս էին նետվում խաղաղասէր շինականները բահերով եւ բրիչներով: Կինը, մանուկը գրկած, հետեւում էր ամուսնուն:

Ո՞ւր էին շտապում:—Իրանք եւս չը գիտէին: Զանգակները հնչում էին: Եկեղեցու ձայնը կոչում էր նրանց:

Մի տեղ մռայլ կույտի նման նշմարվում էր անորոշ մթութիւն: Շինականները դիմում էին դէպի այն կողմը: Հեռուից փոքր էր երեւում կույտը, բայց որքան մօտենում էին, նա աճում էր, ընդարձակվում էր եւ մարդիկների բազմութեան էր նմանում:

Ամեն կողմից դիմում էին դէպի այդ կենտրոնը: Դա ամբոխի այն արբեցեալ դրութիւնն էր, երբ վայրենի բնազդումները հրեշաւոր բորբոքման են հասնում, եւ նա այլեւս ինքն իրան հաշիւ չէ տալիս, այլ իբրեւ մի մոլեգնած հեղեղ, առաջ է մղվում, եւ զազանային անգթութեամբ խորտակում է, ոչնչացնում է ամեն ինչ, որ պատահում է նրա ճանապարհի վրա:

Դամկի կատաղութիւնը աւելի սարսափելի կերպարանք է ստանում, երբ նրան առաջնորդում է կղերը,—երբ գործի մէջ խառնվում է կրօնական մոլեռանդութիւնը: Այդ դէպքում վայրենութիւնը սրբագործվում է եկեղեցու եւ Աստուծոյ անունով: Նոյն մոլեռանդութիւնը ստեղծեց ամօթալի ինկվիզիցիան եւ բազմացրեց աու-դո-դաֆէների թիւը:

Այստեղ կատարվում էր նոյնպէս մի աւ-
դողաֆէ: Բայց այրում էին ոչ թէ կենդանի մարդիկ, այլ անշունչ առարկաներ:

Հրապարակի վրա վառվում էր խարոյկը:
Հոգեւորականութիւնը շրջապատել էր նրան:
Թանձր ծուխը բարձրանում էր փայտակոյտից
եւ, տարածվելով ու սեւ ամպերի նման պատե-
լով սեւաջգեստ աբեղաների խումբը, պատկե-
րացնում էր մի մթին կոլորիտ, որ խիստ յատ-
կանիշ էր այն սեւ գործին, որը պատրաստվում
էր կատարվել:

Խարոյկի մի կողմում դիզված էին գրքեր:
Աբեղաներից մէկը կարդաց նզովքը, յետոյ վե-
րառեց գրքերից մէկը եւ նետեց փայտակոյտի
վրա: Միւսները հետեւեցին նրա օրինակին:
Մագաղաթը, կենդանի ողջակէզի նման, սկսեց
խանձվել, սկսեց այրվել: Եւ մի մեծ մարդու
դարեւոր աշխատութիւնները մի քանի րոպէի մէջ
մոխիր դարձան...

Ռամկի ուրախութեան աղաղակը թնդա-
ցրեց օրը: Ամեն բերանից լսելի էր լինում,
«ազատվեցա՜նք ագանդաւորի գրքերից... այլեւս
մեր երկրում ցաւ, ժանտախտ, երաշտութիւն չի
լինի...»:

Դրանով չվերջացաւ ռամկի սնահաւա-
տութիւնը եւ կղերի հալածասիրութիւնը:—Մնում
էր՝ ցաւի, ժանտախտի, երաշտութեան եւ այլ
զանազան պատուհասների ծագման մի այլ աղ-

բիւր:—Այն եւս պետք էր ողչացնել:

Ռամկի բազմութիւնը խուռն հոսանքով սկսեց ընթանալ դէպի մի այլ կողմ: Ընդհանուր աղմուկի եւ աղաղակների շփոթութեան մէջ ոչինչ չէր հասկացվում: Բոլորին տիրել էր մի տեսակ կատաղի հիւանդոտ ոգեւորութիւն: Նըրանք շրջապատեցին մի անշուք գերեզման, որ պատած էր մացառներով: Աբեղաներից մէկը առաջին օրինակը տուեց, առեց բրիչը, սկսեց բրել: Բազմաթիւ բահեր եւ բրիչներ հետեւեցին նրա օրինակին: Մի քանի րոպէի մէջ գերեզմանը բացվեցաւ: «Ադանդատորի» մարմնի նըշխարները լեցրին պարկերի մէջ: Կանայքը մի առանձին եռանդով գերեզմանի հողն էին աձում իրանց գոգնոցների եւ հագուստի ծրոշակների մէջ: Բոլորը մաքրեցին, բոլորը հաւաքեցին: Գերեզմանի հետքն անգամ չը մնաց: Յետոյ ցնծութեան աղաղակներով հանդիսաւոր թափորը դիմեց դէպի մերձակայ գետը: «Ադանդատորի» ոսկերքը եւ նրա գերեզմանի փոշին աձեցին գետի մէջ: Ալիքները ծփացին, գետը շարունակեց իր խաղաղ հոսանքը եւ կոդերի հալածասիրութեան գոռը ծածկեց իր սառն կոհակների տակ...

Այդ—Մովսէս Խորենացու մարմնի փըրանքն էր:

Նոյն միջոցին, երբ կատարվում էր այդ ամoթալի գործը, մի երիտասարդ աբեղայ, միայնակ կանգնած մի բարձրաւանդակի վրա,

հեռուից նայում էր։ Որպէս մարմնացած սրրտ-
մտութիւն, խորին վրդովմունքով նայում էր նա,
եւ նրա դողդոջուն շրթունքներից դուրս էին թռռ-
չում հետեւեալ խօսքերը։

—Խաւարի՛ զաւակնե՛ր... մեր նորածին գր-
րականութեան այդ բազմավաստակ մշակին
դուք հալածեցիք նրա ամբողջ կենդանութեան
ժամանակ։ Նրա ծերութիւնը անցաւ ցաւերով եւ
դառնութեամբ։ Գերեզմանի մէջ միայն նա պէտք
է հանգստութիւն գտնէր։ Իսկ այդ հանգստու-
թիւնից եւս զրկեցիք նրան... Ապագայ սերունդը
անեծքով եւ նզովքով կը դրոշմէ ձեր անիրաւ
վարմունքը... Իսկ Նա՛, որի յիշատակը դուք աշ-
խատեցիք ջնջել աշխարհի երեսից,—Նա յաւիտեան անմահ կը մնայ իրաքանչիւր հայի սրտում...

Այդ բողոքողը Խորենացու աշակերտ Յուսիկն էր։[22]

---

22 Գրելով «Պարոյր Հայկազն», մենք թոյլ տուեցինք մեզ մի
փոքրիկ անախրոնզմ անել, որպէս զի Պարոյրի եւ Խորենացու ժամանակները մօտեցնենք միմեանց, թէեւ շատ հեռու
չեն։ Իսկ պատմական ճշտութիւնները պահպանեցինք, որքան ներելի է բանաստեղծութեան մէջ։ Մեր աշխատութեան
միայն համառօտութիւնը տպուեցաւ «Աղբիւրի» մէջ, իսկ նրա
ընդարձակը կը տպուի առանձին գրքոյկով։

THE LIFE OF PROHAERESIUS

EUNAPIUS

*(TRANSLATED AND ANNOTATED BY
WILMER C. WRIGHT)*

Julian of Cappadocia, the sophist, flourished in the time of Aedesius, and was a sort of tyrant at Athens. For all the youths from all parts flocked to him, and revered the man for his eloquence and his noble disposition. For there were indeed certain other men, his contemporaries, who in some degree attained to the comprehension of true beauty and reached the heights of his renown, namely Apsines of Lacedaemon who won fame as a writer on rhetoric, and Epagathus, and a whole host of names of that sort. But Julian surpassed them all by his great genius, and he who was second to him was a bad second. He had numerous pupils who came, so to speak, from all parts of the world, and when dispersed in every country were admired wherever and whenever they established themselves. But most distinguished of them all were the inspired Prohaeresius, Hephaestion, Epiphanius of Syria, and Diophantus the Arab. It is fitting that I should also mention Tuscianus, since he too was one of Julian's pupils, but I have already spoken of him in my account of the reign of the Emperor Julian.[1] The author himself saw Julian's house at Athens; poor and humble as it was, nevertheless from it breathed the fragrance of Hermes and the Muses, so closely did it resemble a holy temple. This

---

1 *i.e.,* in his *Universal History.*

house he had bequeathed to Prohaeresius. There, too, were erected statues of the pupils whom he had most admired; and he had a theatre of polished marble made after the model of a public theatre, but smaller and of a size suitable to a house. For in those days, so bitter was the feud at Athens between the citizens and the young students,[2] as though the city after those ancient wars of hers was fostering within her walls the peril of discord, that not one of the sophists ventured to go down into the city and discourse in public, but they confined their utterances to their private lecture theatres and there discoursed to their students. Thus, they ran no risk of their lives, but there competed for applause and fame for eloquence.

Though I leave much unsaid, I must set down and introduce into this narrative the following sample of all Julian's learning and prudence. It so happened that the boldest of the pupils of Apsines had, in a fierce encounter, got the upper hand of Julian's pupils in the course of the war of factions[3]

2　The undying antagonism of "Town" and "Gown" was probably intensified by religious differences, since most of the students were opposed to Christianity.

3　The faction fights of the sophists and their pupils are often mentioned by Libanius ; *cf.* Himerius, *Oration* iv. 9, and his *Oration* xix., which is addressed to those pupils who are so occupied with these encounters that they neglect their lectures. The incident here described with lively interest by Eunapius had occurred seventy years before he wrote the *Lives*.

that they kept up. After laying violent hands on them in Spartan fashion,[4] though the victims of their ill-treatment had been in danger of their lives, they prosecuted them as though they themselves were the injured parties. The case was referred to the proconsul, who, showing himself stern and implacable, ordered that their teacher also be arrested, and that all the accused be thrown into chains, like men imprisoned on a charge of murder. It seems, however, that, for a Roman, he was not uneducated or bred in a boorish and illiberal fashion. Accordingly, Julian was in court, as he had been ordered, and Apsines was there also, not in obedience to orders but to help the case of the plaintiffs. Now all was ready for the hearing of the case, and the plaintiffs were permitted to enter. The leader of the disorderly Spartan faction was one Themistocles, an Athenian, who was in fact responsible for all the trouble, for he was a rash and headstrong youth and a disgrace to his famous name. The proconsul at once glared fiercely at Apsines, and said: "Who ordered you to come here?" He replied that he had come because he was anxious about his children. The magistrate concealed his real opinion and said no more; and then the prisoners who had been so unfairly treated again came before the

---

4 Spartan violence, *Laconica manus,* was apparently a proverb, but here there is a further allusion to the nationality of Apsines.

court, and with them their teacher. Their hair was uncut and they were in great physical affliction, so that even to the judge they were a pitiful sight. Then the plaintiffs were permitted to speak, and Apsines began to make a speech, but the proconsul interrupted him and said: "This procedure is not approved by the Romans. He who delivered the speech for the prosecution at the first hearing must try his luck at the second also." There was then no time for preparation because of the suddenness of the decision. Now Themistocles had made the speech for the prosecution before, but now on being compelled to speak he changed colour, bit his lips in great embarrassment, looked furtively towards his comrades, and consulted them in whispers as to what they had better do. For they had come into court prepared only to shout and applaud vociferously their teacher's speech in their behalf. Therefore, profound silence and confusion reigned, a general silence in the court and confusion in the ranks of the accusers. Then Julian, in a low and pitiful voice said: "Nay, then, give me leave to speak." Whereupon, the proconsul exclaimed: "No, not one of you shall plead, you teachers who have come with your speeches prepared, nor shall anyone of your pupils applaud the speaker; but you shall learn forthwith how perfect and how pure is the justice that the Romans dispense. First let Themistocles finish his speech for the prosecution, and then he whom you think best fitted shall speak in defence." But no one spoke up for the plaintiffs, and Themistocles was a scandal and a disgrace to his great name. When, thereupon, the proconsul ordered that anyone who could should reply to the earlier speech of the prosecution, Julian the sophist said: "Proconsul, in your superlative justice you have transformed Apsines into a Pythagoras, who tardily but very properly has learned how to maintain silence; for Pythagoras long ago (as you are well aware) taught his pupils the Pythagorean manner. But, if you allow one of my pupils to make our defence, give orders for Prohaeresius to be released from his bonds, and you shall judge for yourself whether I have taught him the Attic manner or the Pythagorean." The proconsul granted this request very graciously, as Tuscianus,[5] who was present at the trial, reported to the author, and Prohaeresius came forward from the ranks of the defendants without his fetters before them all, after his master had called out to him not in a loud and piercing voice, such as is used by those who

____

5 Tuscianus, who must have been very old when Eunapius knew him, was a correspondent of Libanius; he held various offices in the East and was for a time a colleague of Anatolius in the government of Illyricum.

exhort and incite athletes contending for a garland, but still in penetrating accents: "Speak, Prohaeresius! Now is the time to make a speech!" He then first delivered a prooemium of some sort. Tuscianus could not exactly recall it, though he told me its purport. It launched out and soon slid into a pitiable account of their sufferings and he inserted an encomium of their teacher. In this prooemium he let fall only one allusion to a grievance, when he pointed out how headlong the proconsular authority had been, since not even after sufficient proof of their guilt was it proper for them to undergo and suffer such treatment. At this the proconsul bowed his head and was overcome with admiration of the force of his arguments, his weighty style, his facility and sonorous eloquence. Meanwhile they all longed to applaud, but sat cowering as though forbidden to do so by a sign from heaven, and a mystic silence pervaded the place. Then he lengthened his speech into a second prooemium as follows (for this part Tuscianus remembered): "If, then, men may with impunity commit any injustice and bring accusations and win belief for what they say, before the defence is heard, so be it! Let our city be enslaved to Themistocles!" Then up jumped the proconsul, and shaking his purple-edged cloak (the Romans call it a "tebennos"[6]), that austere and inexorable judge applauded Prohaeresius like a schoolboy. Even Apsines joined in the applause, not of his own free will, but because there is no fighting against necessity. Julian his teacher could only weep. The proconsul ordered all the accused, but of the accusers their teacher only, to withdraw, and then, taking aside Themistocles and his Spartans, he reminded them forcibly of the floggings of Lacedaemon, and added besides the kind of flogging in vogue at Athens. Julian himself won a great reputation by his own eloquence, and also through the fame of his disciples, and when he died at Athens he left to his pupils a great occasion for competing over his funeral oration.

—

Of **Prohaeresius** I have said enough in the above narrative, and have set forth his life still more fully in my historical commentaries. Yet it is convenient here and now to go over the facts in more precise detail, seeing that I had unerring knowledge of him and was admitted to his conversation and teaching. And that

---

6   Eunapius gives the Greek word used by the Romans for the *toga* or *trabea*. For the gesture as a sign of approval *cf.* Philostratus, *Lives of the Sophists* (Heliodorus) 626.

is a very great privilege, and has immense power to excite the gratitude due to a teacher; but
even this great and inexpressible gratitude falls
very far short of what the author owes to Prohaeresius for his intimate friendship. The com-
piler of this book had crossed over from Asia to
Europe and to Athens in the sixteenth year of his
age. Now Prohaeresius had reached his eighty-
seventh year, as he himself stated. At this advanced
age his hair was curly and very thick, and because
of the number of grey hairs it was silvered over and
resembled sea foam. His powers of oratory were
so vigorous, and he so sustained his worn body by
the youthfulness of his soul, that the present writer regarded him as an ageless and immortal being,
and heeded him as he might some god who had
revealed himself unsummoned and without cere-
mony. Now it happened that the writer arrived at
the Piraeus about the first watch, and on the voy-
age had been attacked by a raging fever; and several other persons, his relatives, had sailed over with
him. At that time of night, before any of the usual proceedings could take place[7] (for the ship belonged to Athens and many used to lie in wait for
her arrival at the dock, mad enthusiasts each for his

____

7 A reference to the competition of the pupils who lay in wait for
new arrivals and kidnapped them for their own sophists. Here the
captain kidnaps them all for Prohaeresius.

own particular school), the captain went straight on to Athens. The rest of the passengers walked, and the writer, too feeble to walk, was nevertheless supported by them in relays, and so was conveyed to the city. It was by then deepest midnight, at the season when the sun makes the nights longer by retiring farther to the South; for he had entered the sign of Libra,[8] and the night watches[9] were long. The captain, who was an old-time friend and guest of Prohaeresius, knocked at his door and ushered in all this crowd of disciples, so many in fact that, at a time when battles were being fought to win only one or two pupils, the newcomers seemed enough in themselves to man all the schools of the sophists. Some of these youths were distinguished for physical strength, some had more bulky purses, while the rest were only moderately endowed. The author, who was in a pitiable state, had most of the works of the ancient writers by heart, his sole possession.[10] Forthwith there was great rejoicing in the house, and men and women alike ran to and fro, some laughing, others bandying jests. Prohaeresius

---

8   *i.e.* it was the autumnal equinox.

9   The exact meaning is doubtful. Νυκτερεῖον is found only here and may mean "a lodging for the night." Then the sentence would mean that to stay at an inn at the Piraeus would cause delay.

10   Others understand μόνον to be self-depreciatory, i.e. Eunapius could recite, but did not understand them. But nearly always when he uses the phrase ἐπὶ στόματος it implies praise.

at that time of night sent for some of his own relatives and directed them to take in the newcomers. He was himself a native of Armenia, that is to say he came from that part of Armenia which borders most closely on Persia, and these kinsmen of his were named Anatolius and Maximus. They welcomed the new arrivals, and led them to the houses of neighbours and to the baths, and showed them off in every way; and the other students made the usual demonstrations with jokes and laughter at their expense.[11] The rest, once they had been to the baths, were let off and went their way, but the writer, as his sickness grew more severe, was wasting away without seeing Prohaeresius or Athens, and all that he so desired seemed to have been only a dream. Meanwhile his own relatives and those who had come from Lydia were greatly concerned; and as all men are prone to attribute greater talent to those who are leaving us in the flower of their youth, they told many surprising falsehoods about him, and conspired to invent prodigious fictions, so that the whole city was overwhelmed by extraordinary grief, as though for some great calamity. But a certain Aeschines, not an Athenian, for Chios was his birthplace, who had slain many, not

____

11 This was part of the regular "hazing" or "ragging" of the novices by the older pupils, described by Libanius and others; cf. Gregory Nazianzen, Oration xix. 328B.

only those whom he had undertaken to cure but also those whom he had merely looked at, called out in the midst of my sorrowing friends, as became known later: "Come, allow me to give medicine to the corpse." And so they gave Aeschines permission to murder those too who were already dead. Then he held my lips apart with certain instruments and poured in a drug; what it was he revealed afterwards, and the god many years later bore witness thereto; at any rate he poured it in, and the patient's stomach was at once expurged, he opened his eyes to the light and recognized his own people. Thus Aeschines by this single act buried his past errors and won reverence both from him who had been delivered from death and from those who rejoiced at his deliverance. For so great an achievement he was worshipped by all, and he then crossed over to Chios, only waiting long enough to give the patient more of that strong medicine, that he might recover his strength; and thus he who had been preserved became the intimate friend of his preserver.

Now the divine Prohaeresius had not yet beheld the author, but he too had mourned for him almost as though he were dead, and when he was told of this unexpected and unheard-of recovery he sent for the best and most distinguished of his pupils and those who had proved the strength of their muscles, and said to them: "I was anxious for this boy who has recovered, though I have not yet seen him; nevertheless, I grieved when he was on the point of death. Now if you wish to do me a favour, initiate him in the public bath, but refrain from all teasing and joking, and scrub him gently as though he were my own son." Thus then it came about, and a fuller account will be given when the author describes the times in which Prohaeresius lived. Yet though the author asserts that all that happened to Prohaeresius was under the direction of some divine providence, he will not in his zeal for the man depart in any way whatsoever from the truth about him, seeing that Plato's saying is fixed and sure, that truth for gods and men alike is the guide to all good.[12]

The physical beauty of Prohaeresius (for my narrative must now return to him) was so striking, even though he was then an old man, that one may well doubt whether anyone had ever been so handsome, even in the flower of youth, and one may marvel also that in a body so tall as his, the power of beauty sufficed to model a shape so admirable in all respects. His height was greater than anyone would be inclined to believe, in fact one would hardly guess it correctly. For he seemed to stand

---

12 Plato, *Laws* 730 b, Oration vi. 188 b.

nine feet high, so that he looked like a colossus when one saw him near the tallest men of his own time. When he was a young man, fate forced him to leave Armenia and transferred him to Antioch. He did not desire to visit Athens immediately, since he was embarrassed by lack of means; for he was unlucky in this respect, though he was well born. At Antioch he hastened to Ulpian,[13] who was the principal teacher of rhetoric there, and on his arrival he at once ranked with the foremost pupils. When he had studied with Ulpian for a long time, he held on his way to Athens and to Julian with the greatest determination, and again at Athens he gained the first place. Hephaestion accompanied him, and these two were devoted friends and rivalled one another in their poverty, just as they were rivals for the highest honours in rhetoric. For instance, they had between them only one cloak and one threadbare mantle and nothing more, and, say, three or four rugs which in the course of time had lost their original dye and their thickness as well. Their only resource therefore was to be two men in one, just as the myths say that Geryon was made up of three bodies; so these students were two men in one.For when Prohaeresius appeared in public, Hephaestion remained invisible and lay under the

______

13 Not the jurist, but a sophist who lived under Constantine.

rugs in bed while he studied the art of rhetoric. Prohaeresius did the same when Hephaestion appeared abroad; in such poverty did they both live.

Nevertheless, Julian's soul leaned towards Prohaeresius, his ears were on the alert to listen to him, and he was awed by the nobility of his genius. And when Julian had departed this life, and Athens desired to choose a successor of equal ability to teach rhetoric, many others gave in their names for this influential sophistic chair, so many that it would be tedious even to write them down. But by the votes of all there were approved and selected Prohaeresius, Hephaestion, Epiphanius, and Diophantus. Sopolis also was added, from a class of men that was of no account but was merely supplementary and despised; and also a certain Parnasius who was of still humbler rank. For in accordance with the Roman law there had to be at Athens many to lecture and many to hear them. Now when these had been elected, the humbler men were sophists only in name, and their power was limited to the walls of their lecture rooms and the platform on which they appeared. But the city at once took sides with the more influential, and not only the city but all the nations under the rule of Rome, and their quarrels did not concern oratory alone, for they strove to maintain the credit of whole nations for oratorical talent. Thus, the East[14] manifestly fell to the lot of Epiphanius, Diophantus was awarded Arabia, while Hephaestion, overawed by Prohaeresius, forsook Athens and the society of men; but the whole Pontus and its neighbouring peoples sent pupils to Prohaeresius, admiring the man as a marvel that their own country had produced. So, too, did all Bithynia and the Hellespont, and all the region that extends beyond Lydia through what is now called Asia as far as Caria and Lycia, and is bounded by Pamphylia and the Taurus. Nay the whole of Egypt also came into his exclusive possession and under his sway as a teacher of rhetoric, and also the country that stretches beyond Egypt towards Libya and is the limit to known and inhabited parts. All this, however, I have stated in the most general terms, for, to speak precisely, there were a few students who were exceptions in these national divisions, because they had either migrated from one teacher to another, or sometimes one had originally been deceived and gone to a teacher other than he had intended. Now a great and violent quarrel arose on account of the extraordinary genius of Prohaeresius, and the faction of all the other sophists so gained the upper hand that they drove him

---

14 *i.e.* Mesopotamia and Syria.

from Athens into exile by bribing the proconsul; and so they themselves held sway over the domain of oratory. But after being driven into exile, and that in the utmost poverty, like Peisistratus he came back again. But the latter had wealth to aid him, while for Prohaeresius his eloquence sufficed, even as Hermes in Homer escorted Priam to the hut of Achilles, though it was in the midst of his foes. Good luck also came to his aid by placing at the head of affairs a younger proconsul who was indignant at the report of what had taken place. So, as the proverb says, "heads became tails,"[15] and with the emperor's permission he returned to Athens from exile; whereupon his enemies for the second time coiled and twisted themselves and reared their heads to attack him, framing other devices against him to suit any future emergencies. They busied themselves with these plots, but meanwhile his friends were beforehand and were smoothing the path of his return, and when Prohaeresius came back (a precise account of all this was given me by an eyewitness, Tuscianus of Lydia, who would have been a Prohaeresius, had not Prohaeresius existed); when, I say, he did return, like some Odysseus arriving home after a long absence, he found a few of his friends safe and sound (among whom was Tus-

____

15 A proverb used by Plato, *Phaedrus* 241 B, and derived from the game ὀστρακίνδα.

cianus), and these looked to him for aid after this incredible miracle. Filled with good hopes on finding them there, he said: "Wait for the proconsul to come." The latter came sooner than could have been believed possible. On his arrival at Athens, he called a meeting of the sophists, and by this means threw all their plans into confusion. They assembled slowly and reluctantly, and since they had to obey the voice of necessity they discussed, each according to his ability, certain questions that were proposed to them, while they were provided with applause by persons who had received their instructions and had been invited for the purpose. Then the meeting broke up, and the friends of Prohaeresius felt discouraged. But the proconsul summoned them a second time, as though to award them honours, ordered them all to be detained, and suddenly he called in Prohaeresius. So they arrived, not knowing what was going to happen. But the proconsul called out: "I wish to propose a theme for you all, and to hear you all declaim on it this very day. Prohaeresius also will speak, either after you or in what order you please." When they openly demurred and, after much consideration and effort, quoted the saying of Aristeides (for it would never do for them to utter anything original); when after all they did produce it, saying that their custom was "not to vomit but to elaborate every theme,"[16] the proconsul exclaimed again with a loud voice: "Speak, Prohaeresius." Then from his chair the sophist first delivered a graceful prelude by way of preliminary speech, in which he extolled the greatness of extempore eloquence, then with the fullest confidence he rose for his formal discussion. The proconsul was ready to propose a definition for the theme, but Prohaeresius threw back his head and gazed all-round the theatre. And when he saw that his enemies were many while his friends were few, and were trying to escape notice, he was naturally somewhat discouraged. But as his guardian deity began to warm to the work and to aid him by playing its part, he again surveyed the scene, and beheld in the farthest row of the audience, hiding themselves in their cloaks, two men, veterans in the service of rhetoric, at whose hands he had received the worst treatment of all, and he cried out: "Ye gods! There are those honourable and wise men! Proconsul, order them to propose a theme for me. Then perhaps they will be convinced that they have behaved impiously." Now the men, on hearing this, slunk away into the crowd that was seated there and did their best to avoid detection. But the proconsul sent some of his soldiers and brought them

16 This saying of Aristeides is quoted by Philostratus, *Lives of the Sophists* 583; it became a proverb.

into full view. After a brief sort of exhortation he appointed them to propose a theme involving the precise definition of terms.[17] Whereupon, after considering for a short time and consulting together, they produced the hardest and most disagreeable theme that they knew of, a vulgar one, moreover, that gave no opening for the display of fine rhetoric. Prohaeresius glared at them fiercely, and said to the proconsul: "I implore you to grant me the just demands that I make before this contest." On his replying that Prohaeresius should not fail to have what was just and fair, the latter said: "I ask to have shorthand writers[18] assigned to me, and that they take their place in the centre of the theatre; I mean men who every day take down the words of Themis,[19] but who today shall devote themselves to what I have to say." The proconsul gave his permission for the most expert of the scribes to come forward, and they stood on either side of Prohaeresius ready to write, but no one knew what he meant to do. Then he said: "I shall ask for something even more difficult to grant." He was told to name it, and said: "There must be no applause

---

17   Hermogenes, *On Invention* iii. 13, gives 5 kinds of ὅρος, "definition"; the kind of argumentation required for each kind was elaborate and technical; it was part of the exposition of the case, the *constitutio definitiva*; *cf.* Quintilian 7:3.
18   Lit. "rapid scribes," sometimes called ταχυγράφοι.
19   The goddess of the law courts.

whatever." When the proconsul had given all present an order to this effect under pain of the severest penalties, Prohaeresius began his speech with a flood of eloquence, rounding every period with a sonorous phrase, while the audience, which perforce kept a Pythagorean silence, in their amazed admiration broke through their restraint, and overflowed into murmurs and sighs. As the speech grew more vehement and the orator soared to heights which the mind of man could not describe or conceive of, he passed on to the second part of the speech and completed the exposition of the theme. But then, suddenly leaping in the air like one inspired, he abandoned the remaining part, left it undefended, and turned the flood of his eloquence to defend the contrary hypothesis. The scribes could hardly keep pace with him, the audience could hardly endure to remain silent, while the mighty stream of words flowed on. Then, turning his face towards the scribes, he said: "Observe carefully whether I remember all the arguments that I used earlier." And, without faltering over a single word, he began to declaim the same speech for the second time. At this the proconsul did not observe his own rules, nor did the audience observe the threats of the magistrate. For all who were present licked the sophist's breast as though it were the statue of some god; some kissed his feet, some his hands, others declared him to be a god or the very model of Hermes, the god of eloquence.[20] His adversaries, on the other hand, lay in the dust eaten up with envy, though some of them even from where they lay could not refrain from applauding; but the proconsul with his whole bodyguard and the notables escorted him from the theatre. After this no one dared to speak against him, but as though they had been stricken by a thunderbolt, they all admitted that he was their superior. However, sometime after, they recovered themselves, like the heads of the Hydra, and were restored to their natural dispositions and reared up their heads; so they tempted certain of the most powerful men in the city by means of costly banquets and smart maidservants, just as kings do when they have been defeated in a regular pitched battle, and in their difficulties are driven to extreme measures, so that they have recourse to light-armed forces and slingers, troops without heavy armour and their inferior reserves; for if they valued these not at all before they are forced to do so now. Just so those sophists, fleeing in their panic to such allies as they could muster, framed their plots, which were base indeed but the men were not to be envied, nor are any who love themselves fatuously. At any rate they had a

______

20 This phrase, first used by Aristeides to describe Demosthenes, became a sophistic commonplace; *cf.* Julian, *Oration* vii. 237 c.

crowd of adherents, and the plot proceeded so that they could reckon on success. However, the genius of Prohaeresius seemed to possess a sort of tyranny over men's minds, and the power of his eloquence to have extraordinary good fortune. For either all intelligent men chose him as their teacher, or those who had attended his school forthwith became intelligent, because they had chosen Prohaeresius.

Now in these days the throng at the imperial court produced a man who passionately desired both fame and eloquence. He came from the city of Berytus and was called Anatolius.[21] Those who envied him nicknamed him Azutrion,[22] and what that name means I leave to that miserable band of mummers to decide! But Anatolius who desired fame and eloquence achieved both these things. For first he won the highest distinction in what is called the science of law, as was natural since his birthplace was Berytus, the foster-mother of all such studies.[23] Then he sailed to Rome where, since his wisdom and eloquence were elevated and weighty, he made his way to court. There he

---

21 Himerius addresses a speech, *Eclogue* 32, to this Anatolius, the prefect of Illyricum; he visited Athens about 345.

22 No explanation of this word is to be found. Such nicknames were common in the fourth century, and the fashion flourished till by the sixth century they are almost surnames and in regular use.

23 Berytus (Beirut) was, as Libanius describes, famous for its school of Roman law. When the youths began to flock thither instead of to the Greek sophists the decay of Greek letters was inevitable.

soon obtained the highest rank, and after holding every high office and winning a great reputation in many official positions (and indeed even his enemies admired him), he finally attained to the rank of pretorian prefect, a magistracy which, though it lacks the imperial purple, exercises imperial power. He had now attained to a fortune in accord with his lofty ambition (for the district called Illyricum had been assigned to him), and since he was devout in offering sacrifices to the gods and peculiarly fond of Greek studies, in spite of the fact that the main current was setting in other directions, instead of choosing as he might have done to visit the most important places in his dominion and administer everything according to his pleasure, he was overcome by a sort of golden madness of desire to behold Greece, and, supported by his distinguished reputation, to turn into realities the mere images of eloquence derived from his learning, and to see for himself what had been an intellectual concept received from such presentation of eloquence as ancient writings could give. He therefore hastened to Greece. Moreover, he sent to the sophists beforehand a certain problem[24] for them to consider, and bade them all practise declaiming on this same problem. All the Greeks marvelled at

---

24 Or "proposition," Latin *quaestio.*

him when they heard of his wisdom and learning and that he was unswervingly upright and incorruptible. Then they set themselves to consider his problem and plotted every day to outwit one another. Nevertheless, since necessity constrained them, they did meet together, and after bringing forward many opposing theories among themselves as to what is called the constitution of the problem (the author never knew of anything so ridiculous as this problem), they were in complete disagreement one with another, since each man in his vanity lauded his own theory and jealously maintained it in the presence of the students. But since Anatolius descending on Greece was more formidable than the famous Persian expedition, that oft-told tale, and the danger stared not indeed all the Greeks but the sophists in the face, all the others (among whom was included a certain Himerius, a sophist from Bithynia; the author knew him only from his writings) toiled and spared no pains or effort, as each one studied the constitution of the theme that he approved. In this crisis Prohaeresius, who trusted in his genius, offended them deeply because he neither showed ambition nor published his secret theory. But now Anatolius was at hand and had made his entry into Athens. When he had with great courage offered sacrifices[25] and formally visited all the temples, as the divine ordinance commanded, he summoned the sophists to the competition. When they were in his presence, they one and all strove to be the first to declaim; so prone to self-love is man! But Anatolius laughed at the boy pupils who were applauding them, and commiserated the fathers whose sons were being educated by such men. Then he called on Prohaeresius who alone was left. Now he had cultivated the acquaintance of one of the friends of Anatolius who knew all the circumstances, and had learned from him the constitution of the theme that Anatolius approved. (This is what the author called ridiculous in what he said above.) And even though the theme was unworthy of consideration, and it was not right that the view of Anatolius should prevail, nevertheless Prohaeresius, when his name was called, obeyed the summons promptly, and modelled his disputation on the constitution of the theme that I have mentioned, and his argument was so able and so elegant that Anatolius jumped up from his seat, the audience shouted applause till they burst, and every man there regarded him as a divine being. Accordingly, Anatolius openly showed him peculiar honour, though he would hardly admit the others

____

25 This was a courageous act because Christian emperors, Constantius and Constans, were on the throne.

to his table. He himself was an accomplished sophist in table-talk and themes suited to a symposium;
hence his symposium was a feast of reason and of
learned conversation. But all this happened many
years ago, and therefore the author has been very
careful in his report of what he learned from hear-
say. Now Anatolius felt great admiration for Milesius also, a man who came from Smyrna in Ionia.
Though fortune had endowed him with the greatest
talents, he abandoned himself to an unambitious
and leisurely life, frequented the temples, neglected
to marry, and cultivated every sort of poetry and
lyric and every kind of composition that is favoured
by the Graces. By this means, then, he won the favour of Anatolius so that he actually called the man
a "Muse." But he used to call the problems raised
by Epiphanius the sophist "Analyses,"[26] making fan
in this way of that teacher's triviality and pedan-
tic accuracy. He satirized all the sophists for their
disagreements over the constitution[27] of a theme,
and said: "If there had been more than thirteen of
these professional sophists, they would no doubt

----

26 Or " Subdivisions," partitioned, arrangement of the speech under headings.

27 The precise meaning of stasis as a rhetorical term is discussed by
the rhetoricians, especially Hermogenes. Cf. Quintiilian ii. 6 where
he says it is the equivalent of the Latin question or constitution or
status. Roughly speaking, it is the "stand" taken by a speaker when
he defines his case. Here, Anatolius implies that there are thirteen
possible stases of the "case" or problem that he had proposed.

have invented still more 'constitutions' in order to declaim on a single problem from every different angle possible." Prohaeresius was the one and only sophist of them all whom he genuinely admired. Now it happened that Prohaeresius had not long before been summoned to the Gallic provinces by Constans, who then held imperial sway, and he had so won over Constans that he sat at his table along with those whom he most honoured. And all the inhabitants of that country who could not attain to a thorough understanding of his lectures and thus admire the inmost secrets of his soul, transferred their wonder and admiration to what they could see plainly before their eyes, and marvelled at his physical beauty and great stature, while they gazed up at him with an effort as though to behold some statue or colossus, so much beyond the measure of man was he in all respects.[28] Moreover, when they observed his abstinence and self-denial they believed him to be passionless and made of iron; for clad in a threadbare cloak and barefooted he re-garded the winters of Gaul as the height of luxury, and he would drink the water of the Rhine when it was nearly freezing. Indeed, he passed his whole life in this fashion, and was never known to touch

28 Here Eunapius seems to imitate Philostratus, *Life of Adrian* 589, where that sophist makes a similar effect on audiences that knew no Greek.

a hot drink. Accordingly, Constans dispatched him to mighty Rome, because he was ambitious to show them there what great men he ruled over. But so entirely did he surpass the ordinary human type that they could select no one peculiarity to admire. So they admired his many great qualities one after another, and were in turn approved by him, and they made and set up in his honour a bronze statue life size with this inscription: "Rome the Queen of cities to the King of Eloquence."[29]

When he was about to return to Athens, Constans permitted him to ask for a present. Thereupon he asked for something worthy of his character, namely several considerable islands that should pay tribute to Athens to provide it with a corn supply. Constans not only gave him these, but added the highest possible distinction by bestowing on him the title of "stratopedarch,"[30] lest any should resent his acquisition of so great a fortune from the public funds. It was necessary for the pretorian prefect to confirm this gift; for the prefect had lately arrived from Gaul. Accordingly, after the competitions in eloquence that I have described, Prohaeresius approached Anatolius and

---

29 Libanius, *Letter* 278, mentions this statue at Rome and another at Athens.

30 This office, originally military, had become that of a Food Controller, cf. Julian, Oration i. 8 c, where he says that Constantine did not disdain it for himself.

begged him to confirm the favour, and summoned not only professional advocates for his cause but almost all the educated men of Greece; for on account of the prefect's visit they were all at Athens. When the theatre was crowded, and Prohaeresius called on his advocates to speak, the prefect ran counter to the expectation of all present, because he wished to test the extempore eloquence of Prohaeresius, and he said: "Speak, Prohaeresius! For it is unbecoming for any other man to speak and to praise the emperor when you are present." Then Prohaeresius, like a war-horse summoned to the plain,[31] made a speech about the imperial gift, and cited Celeus and Triptolemus and how Demeter sojourned among men that she might bestow on them the gift of corn. With that famous narrative he combined the tale of the generosity of Constans, and very speedily he invested the occurrence with the splendour and dignity of ancient legend. Then, as he declaimed, his gestures became more lively, and he displayed all his sophistic art in handling the theme. The fact that he obtained the honour that he asked for shows what his eloquence must have been.

---

31   A proverb; cf. Plato, *Theaetetus* 183d. It is used by Lucian and Julian.

His wife came from Asia, from the city of Tralles, and her name was Amphiclea. They had two little girls, between whose ages there was only so much difference as the time necessary for their conception and birth. But no sooner had they reached that time of life when a child is a wholly lovely and charming thing, and made their father's heart tremble with joy, than they left their parents desolate, both within a few days; so that his grief almost shook Prohaeresius from the reflections that become a philosopher. However, the Muse of Milesius proved able to meet this crisis, and by composing lovely harmonies and expending all his gifts of charm and gaiety he recalled him to reason. When the Romans asked him to send them one of his own pupils, Prohaeresius sent forth Eusebius who was a native of Alexandria. He seemed to be peculiarly suited to Rome, because he knew how to flatter and fawn on the great; while in Athens he was regarded as a seditious person. At the same time Prohaeresius wished to increase his own reputation by sending a man who had been initiated into the sharp practices of political oratory. As for his talent for rhetoric, it is enough to say that he was an Egyptian; for this race passionately loves the poetic arts, whereas the Hermes who inspires serious study has departed from them. He had for an adversary Musonius, who had been his pupil in the sophistic art. (I have for other reasons written about him at length in my Universal History.) When Musonius reared his head to oppose him, Eusebius knew well against what sort of man he had to contend, so he very speedily deserted to take up political oratory.

In the reign of the Emperor Julian, Prohaeresius was shut out of the field of education because he was reputed to be a Christian; and since he observed that the hierophant, like a sort of Delphic tripod, was open to all who had need of him to foretell future events, by strange and wonderful arts he fraudulently intercepted that foreknowledge. For the emperor was having the land measured for the benefit of the Hellenes,[32] to relieve them from oppression in respect of taxes. Thereupon Prohaeresius requested the hierophant[33] to find out from the god whether this benevolence would be permanent. And when he declared that it would not, Prohaeresius learned in this way what the future would bring, and took courage. The author, who had attained at this time to about his sixteenth year, arrived at Athens and was enrolled among his pupils, and Prohaeresius loved him like his own son. Five years later the author was preparing to go to Egypt, but his parents summoned him and compelled him

---

32 Probably "those of the Hellenic faith."
33 *i.e.,* of Eleusis.

to return to Lydia. To become a sophist was the obvious course to which all urged him. Now a few days later Prohaeresius departed this life. He was a great and gifted man, even as I have described, and he filled the whole known world with the fame of his discourses, and with those who had been his pupils.

—

Epiphanius was a native of Syria, and he was reputed to be very skilful in distinguishing and defining controversial themes, but as an orator he was slack and nerveless. Nevertheless, as the rival of Prohaeresius in the sophistic profession he actually attained to great fame. For human beings are not content to admire one man only, but so prone are they to envy, so completely its slave, that when a man excels and towers above the rest, they set up another as his rival; and thus derive their controlling principles from opposites just as in the science of physics. Epiphanius did not live to be old, but died of blood-poisoning, and his wife also, who was an exceedingly handsome woman, met the same fate. They left no children. Epiphanius was not personally known to the author, for he died long before the latter's sojourn in Athens.

—

Diophantus was a native of Arabia who forced his way into the ranks of the professors of rhetoric. That same envious opinion of mankind of which I have just spoken set him up as another rival of Prohaeresius, as though one should oppose Callimachus to Homer. But Prohaeresius laughed all this to scorn, and he refused to give serious thought to human beings and their foibles. The writer knew Diophantus and often heard him declaim in public. But he has not thought fit to quote in this work any of his speeches or what he remembers of them. For this document is a record of noteworthy men; it is not a satire. However it is said that he delivered a funeral oration in honour of Prohaeresius (for the latter died before he did), and they relate that he concluded with these words about Salamis and the war against the Medes: "O Marathon and Salamis, now are ye buried in silence! What a trumpet of your glorious victories have ye lost!"[34] He left two sons who devoted themselves to a luxurious life and money-making.

---

34 *i.e.* Prohaeresius had used these commonplaces effectively.

ACKNOWLEDGEMENTS

We extend our thanks to Ani Dekirmenchyan, and Drs. Minas Kojayan and Robert Bedrosian for their help with certain tricky phrases and passages. Several of the translated footnotes from Ghazar Parpec'i's *History of the Armenians* were also borrowed from Robert Bedrosian's translation.

SOPHENE